# A GIFT TO CHERISH

Gavin Reid and nurse Caroline Drummond, both widowed, are happily anticipating their forthcoming marriage. Gavin has his own business restoring old buildings, and when he has to have an operation, Caroline's son Keith rallies round to keep the business running smoothly. Meanwhile, Gavin's daughter Kate has fallen in love with Angus, a painter, who is a friend of the family. When Gavin recovers, Angus goes to Brazil but, whilst there, he realises just how much he misses Kate . . .

*Books by Jane Carrick*
*in the Linford Romance Library:*

DIAMONDS ON THE LAKE
A PEARL FOR LOVE
A HANDFUL OF MIST
THE COURAGE OF ANNA CAMERON
FACE OF A STRANGER
MY DARLING GERALDINE
GERALDINE'S WAR
LOVE MUST BE SURE
SO GOLDEN THEIR HARVEST
FORSAKING ALL OTHERS

JANE CARRICK

# A GIFT TO CHERISH

*Complete and Unabridged*

## LINFORD
*Leicester*

First published in Great Britain in 1978

First Linford Edition
published 2006

Copyright © 1978 by Jane Carrick

British Library CIP Data

Carrick, Jane
A gift to cherish.—Large print ed.—
Linford romance library
1. Love stories
2. Large type books
I. Title
823.9′14 [F]

ISBN 1–84617–337–X

Published by
F. A. Thorpe (Publishing)
Anstey, Leicestershire

Set by Words & Graphics Ltd.
Anstey, Leicestershire
Printed and bound in Great Britain by
T. J. International Ltd., Padstow, Cornwall

This book is printed on acid-free paper

# All Their Tomorrows

What a beautiful day it had turned out to be, thought Gavin Reid, as he drove out of the gates of Tordale General Hospital, and turned right towards Mornington Road.

He knew that Caroline Drummond would be waiting anxiously to hear the results of his check-up and he wanted to discuss every aspect of the specialist's report with her before driving home to Stronmore.

After all, it was Caroline's concern just as much as his.

The traffic was quiet at this time of day, and Gavin Reid found himself revelling in the beauty of the green leaves against a backdrop of deep blue sky.

It was funny, he mused. But before his illness, he would rarely have noticed such things.

He felt he would never again take the beauty of the countryside for granted. Nor, for that matter, the love of his family — and more especially the love he and Caroline shared.

It was second time round for both of them, but Gavin Reid felt he would always be grateful for her support through the difficult months now behind them.

He recalled his interview with the specialist earlier that afternoon.

'You're making progress, Mr Reid,' the specialist had told him. 'Though I wouldn't advise you to do anything very strenuous for a few months yet. Now, let me see . . . oh yes, you're a cabinet maker.'

'I was a joiner.' Gavin Reid smiled. 'My father started our firm in Stronmore over forty years ago, but I've generally steered the firm towards cabinet making, and renovating old furniture, that sort of thing.'

'You've got someone taking the responsibility off your shoulders. I take it?'

He nodded.

'My future stepson. Keith Drummond. He used to be with a timber firm, but I've persuaded him to come into the business.

'His mother and I . . . well . . . we're planning to marry as soon as I'm fit and well. I believe you know my fiancée. Nurse Drummond?'

Mr Lovell, the specialist, smiled.

'She was a young nurse when I was a junior doctor. She's still nursing here, part time. Well, Mr Reid, if you've got Nurse Drummond to look after you . . . '

'I'm not getting married just to find myself a nurse,' Gavin Reid said, his eyes twinkling.

'That goes without saying.' Mr Lovell smiled. 'Nurse Drummond has done a fine job of bringing up Keith since her husband died. She deserves her happiness, and you're a lucky man. Mr Reid. I see you lost your wife . . . ah . . . '

'Six years ago,' Gavin Reid replied. 'She took viral pneumonia after flu. She was always rather delicate.'

'You've been through a bad time.' Mr Lovell nodded with sympathy.

Gavin Reid felt that the specialist was taking more than the usual interest in him, probably due to Caroline's position in the hospital. The grey eyes were very keen, obviously weighing up the situation carefully.

'And you had planned to marry shortly?'

'Yes. My daughters are all grown up now.'

'Gemma is married, and Kate works in our local post office. Sally . . . ' Mr Reid laughed a little, and shook his head. 'Sally changes her mind about what she wants to do every five minutes, but she's a receptionist at Stronmore Hotel at the moment.'

'She's the youngest?'

'Yes . . . eighteen.'

'No sons then?'

Again Gavin Reid smiled a little.

'I look on Keith Drummond as a son. He's a fine boy.'

4

Suddenly the red light was flashing on Mr Lovell's intercom.

'Well, Mr Reid,' he said, standing up after he had acknowledged the signal. 'Just mind how you go. I've written to your own doctor, but I don't foresee any complications. I hope you and Nurse Drummond will be very happy.'

★   ★   ★

The houses in Mornington Road had nearly all been converted into comfortable flats. Gavin Reid pulled up outside number six and rang the bell.

A moment later Caroline appeared, her blue eyes anxious as she opened the door.

He put an arm around her shoulders as they walked upstairs to her first-floor flat while he told her the good news.

'Mr Lovell thinks I can make plans for the future now, darling,' he told her, after she had settled him into the settee.

She had set a tray for both of them, and she disappeared into the kitchen for a moment to make the tea.

'Maybe it should be champagne,' she called, laughing.

'I'll settle for tea,' he replied. 'I feel as though I'll never again be as happy as I am now.'

Caroline Drummond paused as a shiver ran through her at the words. Gavin seemed almost too happy. Yet she could see no signs of any dark clouds on the horizon.

She remembered the dull, heavy years after Martin died, alleviated only by the energy she put into her work.

Fortunately she'd had Keith to worry about, though there had been little need.

He had always been a plodder, rather like his father, which was mainly why he had sought a job with the timber company, instead of studying for Highers and a university course.

It was through his work that he had first met Gavin Reid, and had, in fact, introduced his mother to the older man.

They'd had time to build up a liking and respect for one another before she came on the scene, and there had been no awkward moments when she told Keith that she and Gavin planned to marry.

Already Gavin looked on Keith as a son and he'd had no hesitation in putting the boy in charge of the business when he had gone into hospital for his operation.

It had been a fine gesture of trust, thought Caroline lovingly, and one which seemed to set the seal of their family, as a unit.

'Keith should be home in another half-hour,' she told Gavin, looking at the clock. 'Will you wait to see him before you go?'

'Of course. I'd better phone Stronmore, too. Kate should be home shortly, and it will settle her mind to know I'm OK.'

Caroline nodded. She was very fond of Gavin's middle daughter, though she privately thought that Sally, the youngest, was a bit spoilt.

Sally was the only member of both families who had not shown genuine delight when she and Gavin had decided to marry. She was too wrapped up in herself, thought Caroline.

Kate, on the other hand, had taken the news quietly at first, then as time passed, her grave little face had begun to relax, and there was a look almost of relief in her eyes. Kate was inclined to take her responsibilities seriously.

Caroline had always wanted a daughter as much as Gavin had wanted a son, and that daughter was surely Kate Reid.

'Would four weeks be too soon?' Gavin asked, after his second cup of tea.

'Four weeks! That's no time at all.'

'Why should we hang about waiting, love? My house at Stronmore is big enough for all of us. It will be handy for Keith, and the girls will be thankful to have it properly run again, I'm sure.

'Mrs Simpson comes up from the village, and she'll be a good help to you.

You won't want to keep on this flat, will you?'

Caroline sighed, and shook her head.

'I had to give up our home after Martin died. I don't think Keith has ever liked this flat. No, I'll be glad to move out of here.'

'Well then . . . '

'All right, darling. A quiet wedding with just the family in four weeks' time.'

Keith's key sounded in the lock, and a moment later he was being welcomed by his mother, and stepfather-to-be. Both were eager to tell him the news.

'That's great,' Keith said, looking slightly overwhelmed, so that the older couple laughed.

'We're behaving like a couple of children,' Gavin Reid said ruefully, 'but you've no idea how wonderful it feels to be back in trim again.'

'Then . . . you'll be wanting to take over the reins again?' Keith asked carefully, as he sat down beside them in front of the fire.

He was rather a quiet, gentle young

man, Gavin Reid thought affectionately, looking into Keith's earnest blue eyes.

'Not for a while yet,' he said genially. 'No, when I put you in, I gave you full charge of the place, Keith. I wouldn't dream of taking that away from you just yet.'

The tension left the boy, and Mr Reid thought he looked tired. However, he was doing well and it was fine experience for a young man.

It was a well-known firm throughout the county and beyond. They'd been lucky in having a team of skilled men working for them, and though some of them had gone, other young men were always coming forward.

More and more, they were being called on to renovate old houses and churches, as well as fine furniture.

Keith's predecessor, Angus Fraser, had done a lot in that line, and now Mr Reid felt it was a heritage to be proud of.

'You look a bit tired, Keith,' Gavin Reid told him. 'You could do with an early night tonight.'

Wasn't the boy more than usually heavy eyed, he wondered. Keith had always seemed to be happy that his mother was planning to marry again, but was he really happy underneath?

He'd been very quiet recently, and now Mr Reid looked at him with speculation. Surely Keith couldn't object to him as a stepfather? He had felt they were as close as any father and son could be.

\* \* \*

The telephone shrilled, and Caroline rose to answer it. They could hear her happy laughter, then Gavin Reid looked guiltily at Keith.

'Oh dear, it's Kate,' he said. 'I meant to ring her, and I forgot.'

Quickly he rose to his feet, and went out to take the receiver from Caroline.

'I'll be home in less than half an hour,' he promised.

'We've been just a bit anxious,' came

Kate's clear voice, then she lowered it a little. 'Mrs Simpson's still here. I think she's determined to stay till she finds out how you got on with your check-up.'

Gavin Reid laughed. Molly Simpson had been helping to look after Hazelbank for years, and she took a lively interest in everything connected with the family.

But he wanted to tell his family his news about the wedding date before Mrs Simpson got to know.

'I'm absolutely OK, dear,' Mr Reid said. 'I'll leave for home in about five minutes.'

'I'll have dinner ready for you,' said Kate.

'Just something light, an omelette maybe.'

'But . . . '

'It's been an exciting day.' Gavin Reid cut short her protests. 'Caroline and I have some news for you, but I'll tell you when I get home. I hope Sally will be in by then, too.'

'I see,' Kate said, and there was warmth in her voice. 'See you then, Dad.'

Kate Reid put down the phone and went back into the kitchen, where Mrs Simpson was slowly buttoning her coat.

'Is the news good, Kate?' she asked, her eyes slightly anxious.

'Very good, Mrs Simpson. Father will have to take it easy for a little while yet, but the operation has been a complete success.'

'Oh, that's fine. I've put a steak pie in the oven. Maybe he'd like a helping when he gets home. Unless he's had his tea?'

'No. I'm sure we'll manage, Mrs Simpson. Sally and I will enjoy the pie, anyway.' Kate glanced at the clock. 'She's a bit late this evening.'

'You can't exactly set the clock by Sally,' said Mrs Simpson.

Kate watched Mrs Simpson until she had closed the garden gate behind her, and turned left towards the village, then she picked up the telephone and dialled her older sister's number.

Gemma had married Alec Johnstone, a young farmer, and was always kept busy, but the milking should be finished by this time.

★  ★  ★

The phone rang for a minute or two, and Kate was about to hang up when the receiver was lifted, and she listened to a few snorts and small breathing noises. She had no difficulty in recognising Norman, her four-year-old nephew.

'Is Mummy there, darling?' Kate asked.

'No,' said Norman. 'She's in the kitchen. Smokey's got three new kittens.'

'How lovely. Perhaps we could have one, Norrie. Can you ask Mummy to come to the phone?'

'No. I've got a hole in my wellies. Daddy says he'll need the vet for Daisy. Cheerio.'

The receiver was slammed back down, and Kate sighed as she turned away.

Norman was growing into a handful for her sister, in addition to all her other work. Suddenly the kitchen door flew open, and Sally hurried in, looking as fresh and pretty as always.

'Hello, Sally. I'm glad you're home before Dad,' said Kate, smiling at her sister. 'He's on his way now. He's got a good report from the hospital.'

'Great,' Sally said, throwing herself on to a chair. 'I'm dead beat. We've had a hectic day at the hotel. All the fishermen are beginning to check in for the season.

'It will be nothing but fishing talk in the lounge for the next three months. I don't know how the wives stand it! Fancy saving up for a holiday, then spending it here, and not in London, or Paris, or Rome.'

'Some people like a quiet country holiday,' said Kate amiably, 'though I do know some people also like London.'

'Such as Angus Fraser?' Sally commented. 'He hasn't seemed to miss the gamekeeper's cottage, or his brother, come to that. And Lachie just walks about the place, contented to be a gamekeeper like his father.

'If I'd been a boy instead of a girl, I wouldn't stay here two minutes.'

'Well, it's a good job we have people like Lachie Fraser,' put in Kate warmly, 'who are willing to follow in their father's footsteps. Being a gamekeeper is an essential job.

'As for Angus . . . well . . . he has other talents just as important and he's developing them in London. He's a wonderful artist. Father always said so.'

'You always leap to the defence of the Frasers,' Sally told her. 'But, then you were always with them, when we were small . . . you and Angus, and now Lachie.

'You're quite content here, whereas I . . . well . . . I get bored, if you must know. There's a new assistant manager starting next week, I bet he's just as dull as all the rest.'

Kate sighed.

'If you took more interest in people,

instead of yourself, you wouldn't find it so dull. And anyway, I expect Father and Caroline will have set the date for their wedding, now that he's OK. I think that's the bit of news he's saving up for us until he gets home.'

Sally's expression didn't lighten.

'I don't think Caroline thinks much of me,' she said morosely. 'I bet she starts trying to reform me as soon as the knot is tied. And we'll likely have Keith come to live with us!'

'Well he's all right. I thought you liked Keith Drummond.'

'He's OK,' said Sally, shrugging. 'Not exactly scintillating. Hold on, Kate, not so much of that pie, pastry is very fattening. Why can't Mrs Simpson make us a decent salad sometimes?'

'We're lucky to have anything prepared at all! Oh . . . good! That's Father's car.'

Kate ran out to meet her father, with Sally following rather more leisurely.

It was good to be home, thought Gavin Reid, as he looked at them.

'Tell us all about it,' Kate invited. She was slender and dark, like her mother, and her dark eyes sparkled with excitement.

'Well, I saw Mr Lovell, and . . . '

'She means the wedding plans.' Sally laughed.

'You're always ahead of me,' their father said. 'All right. Caroline and I have set the date for next month.'

'Goodness, we'll have to get things ready in time.' Kate said.

Sally hadn't said a word. About four weeks, she mused.

'Caroline won't mind if there's a bit of dust,' Mr Reid said confidently. 'It will give her something to do . . . getting to know the house, and so on.'

He was silent for a moment. 'I don't think she'll want to make too many changes.'

'I think she ought to change things to suit herself,' said Kate. 'After all, it will be her home, too.'

'Are you having a big wedding?' Sally asked. 'Will you want the reception at the hotel?'

18

'I would think Caroline will want it to be fairly quiet.' Mr Reid said. 'Mainly the family and a few friends.'

'What about Angus?' Kate asked eagerly. 'Lachie will be going, I expect, but do you think Angus will come home?'

Mr Reid looked into her shining eyes. Kate had always tended to hero-worship Angus Fraser.

'He might,' he agreed carefully. 'You never know.'

'I'll get your omelette,' Kate said and hurried away to the kitchen.

Sally decided she had to wash her hair.

\* \* \*

Gavin Reid was left alone, his mind still on the Fraser boys. From his seat by the fireside, he could look up to the white-painted game-keeper's cottage, perched on the hillside, where Angus and Lachie had been born.

They had been in and out of

Hazelbank all their lives, playing with his own three girls.

Lachie was Kate's age, but Angus a little older, though even as a boy he had shown gentleness and understanding with the girls, and had helped them home many a time with skinned knees and scratched legs.

Angus had spent a great deal of his time drawing and painting. Mr Reid remembered one occasion when Angus had called in at the workshop while he was renovating a set of chairs and a chiffonier.

There had been a piece of wood sculpture depicting a fallow deer in the chiffonier, and Angus had examined it carefully.

'Do you like that, Angus?' he had asked.

'It's very nice, Mr Reid,' the boy said, turning it over in his hands. 'But it isn't really like a proper fallow deer. See . . . '

He took out his sketch book and pencil, and a few moments later he showed Mr Reid the drawing of an animal which looked as though it could walk out of the page.

'It should be broader here, Mr Reid, and the ears aren't set properly, See?'

'I see,' the older man had replied, rather faintly. 'You . . . you're quite an artist, Angus.'

'I just know how to draw things,' the boy said.

Gavin Reid had called in to see Ewan and Mary Fraser a week or two later, and had casually mentioned this gift Angus possessed.

'He could do with going to art college, Ewan,' he said.

'Ach, there's no question of that, Mr Reid,' Ewan said, shaking his head. 'How could we ever send Angus to art college?

'No, he'll just have to keep his painting for high days and holidays, and earn his bread and butter gamekeeping like myself. There's always work for a good gamekeeper.'

Mr Reid watched Mary Fraser turn

away, her face shadowed. Angus took after his mother, with fine bones and soft light brown hair. But though he was tall and thin, he had the lithe strength of an athlete, and no-one could out-run Angus.

'I thought Lachie was the one who wanted to take up gamekeeping?'

'Lachie is young yet, but that's true enough. He loves the life, even if he's inclined to keep himself to himself.'

'What about Angus coming to work for me?' Mr Reid had asked. 'He could serve his apprenticeship, and even if I couldn't offer him an artistic career in fine art, he could help quite a lot with designing furniture. He's got a real feel for creative art.'

Ewan Fraser looked doubtful.

'I don't know, Mr Reid,' he'd said, stroking his chin. 'We've always worked on the land, back to my grandfather's time.'

'We could ask the lad,' Mary Fraser said suddenly.

She had faced her husband quietly

but firmly, and Angus had jumped at the chance.

He had also proved an excellent pupil, thought Mr Reid, his mind going back over the years.

Angus had learned to love wood, and took a pride in the delicate work he undertook.

Stronmore was a quiet place, and the people lived quiet, peaceful lives.

Stronmore Castle had opened out as a hotel with fine fishing as an added attraction and they all grew used to seeing the fishermen around the place.

Angus had kept on drawing wild birds, woodland creatures and even the river itself as it tumbled its way through Stronmore.

As a gamekeeper, Ewan Fraser had to arrange the fishing permits, and one of his clients, Mr Kenneth Morland, called in one day at the cottage and began to study Angus's drawings.

'This boy should be at college,' he said. 'What a waste. He has a lot of talent and skill.'

'He does well enough,' Ewan said. 'He's learning great skills with Mr Reid.'

'Well, he should have his chance,' Mr Morland insisted. 'I'll send him details of a competition. I think he should enter for it. He would stand a good chance of gaining a scholarship to an art college in London.'

Ewan had dismissed the matter from his mind, so that when Angus won the scholarship, he had hardly known what to do for the best. Gavin Reid offered to talk things over with Angus.

Even now, Gavin could see the hope in the boy's sensitive, intelligent face, and he could well understand the longing he had seen there.

That longing had been his own, when he used to help his father knock up a few shelves, when he wanted to design beautiful things, and polish the wood until it shone like a mirror.

It was for these reasons he had decided to help tide Angus over his lean years at college. The only stipulation being that Angus made the most of this opportunity. At first, Angus had taken some persuading.

'But my father would never allow it,' he had argued.

'He'd never know,' countered Gavin Reid. 'It's between you and me. Angus . . . just you and me. Come on now.'

Angus stood up and faced Mr Reid proudly.

'Very well, and thank you. Some day . . . some day I may have the opportunity to pay you back.'

They had shaken hands, and Angus had gone off to London, leaving a great gap in their lives.

\* \* \*

Lachie, his younger brother, had grown into a fine young man, as tall as Angus, but of broader build.

He called regularly for Kate and they often went to local functions together, and even to dances.

'Lachie is coming over in an hour.'

Kate's voice broke into her father's thoughts. She had cooked him a delicious omelette, and he began to eat with enjoyment. 'He just wants to see how you are.'

'That's nice of him. Oh, did you ring Gemma?'

'Yes . . . and got Norman instead. That wee rascal gets worse every day. He thinks every phone call is for him! He just wouldn't go and find Gemma for me. I'll just go and try again.'

This time Kate was lucky, and her older sister's voice sounded tired and depressed when she answered, though it brightened considerably when Kate gave her all the news.

'I'll try to call in on Saturday,' Gemma promised. 'If I can fit it in.'

'You should take things more easily,' Kate told her rather anxiously.

'You don't know what you're talking about,' Gemma said. 'There's more to it than that.'

'What?'

'Oh . . . not just now, Kate. We'll talk

another time. Do you think I could get Norrie into a velvet suit for the wedding?'

'No.' Kate laughed, and they parted on a lighter note.

Nevertheless, Kate's thoughts weren't quite so bright as she turned away. Sooner or later Gemma was going to run into trouble, if she didn't relax a little more.

She had cleared away the supper table when Lachie Fraser knocked lightly on the kitchen door, and pushed it open. Kate had been going to empty the teapot.

'It's still quite fresh. Do you want a cup of tea. Lachie?'

'If one of your home-made biscuits goes with it,' he said. 'So your father has had good news?'

'The best. We're through here planning the wedding.'

She led the way into the sitting-room where Gavin Reid was sitting contentedly by the fireside. He looked up at Lachie with a welcoming smile.

'My daughters would have me in top

hat and tails,' he said, 'but they're in for a disappointment. When I say a quiet wedding, I mean just that.'

'I doubt if a top hat would suit me either,' Lachie said.

'Nonsense,' Kate said. 'You men just won't dress up when you've got the opportunity.'

She sat down beside Lachie.

'Is there any news from Angus?' she asked. 'We're going to send him an invitation, too, you know. He'll come up for the wedding, won't he, Lachie?'

She turned her brilliant eyes on him, then leaned over to arrange a cushion for her father, and Lachie was glad to sit still for a moment before replying.

Why did Kate keep asking about Angus? Why couldn't they forget him for a little while, he wondered.

Not that he had anything against Angus. He was very fond of his older brother, and proud he had won the scholarship. It wasn't everyone who had such a talented brother, Lachie reminded himself.

But Kate, what did she feel about Angus, he wondered. She seemed always to want to be friends with both of them, but deep down Lachie wanted her all to himself.

He had grown to love her deeply, and that love was giving him an insight and sensitivity he had never known before.

He wanted Angus to stay in London, following the career he was carving out for himself, leaving Kate in Stronmore, where she belonged.

'I mean, he'll want to be here, won't he, Lachie?' Kate asked again.

'I don't know,' Lachie said carefully. 'Of course, he was on the phone quite often when Mr Reid was ill, and Mother had to keep giving him progress reports. But I don't know how he is placed for dropping everything and travelling up to Stronmore. It's an awful long way, Kate.'

'I know,' she said rather crossly.

Maybe Angus wouldn't come, and she couldn't blame him if he didn't, but something in her wanted him to be there. It wouldn't seem the same without Angus — and Lachie. They were just like her own family.

★ ★ ★

The next four weeks were so busy that Kate felt she had little time to dwell on anything other than the wedding.

Caroline called to see them on Kate's half-day and found her hard at work, along with Molly Simpson, cleaning out the old cupboard in the hall.

'Gracious, what's all this?' she asked, as Kate withdrew a slightly blackened face from the deepest recesses of the cupboard.

'We've been meaning to do this for years,' she said, her slight figure enveloped in one of Mrs Simpson's large flowered overalls. 'The wedding is just an excuse.'

'I don't know why it can't be left for me,' Caroline said.

'Because I'm ashamed of the rubbish we've collected,' Kate answered frankly.

30

'One roller skate, a broken mirror
. . . we've had our seven years bad luck
. . . and loads of ancient old jam jars.'

'We'll keep those for jam-making,'
Caroline said promptly. 'Why don't you
put it all back, and I'll go through it
later?'

'Let's all have a cup of tea and the
cakes I've brought. Keith will call in
later. He and Gavin are having a bit of a
pow-wow, Kate.'

'Business I expect. He rang Father
up.'

'Yes, he fancies a break for a few days
before the wedding. He's been looking
tired recently.'

'Where's Keith going?' Kate asked.

'London.'

'London! Hey, maybe he'd call in
and see Angus. I'd like to see him up
here for the wedding.'

'Maybe he will.' Caroline laughed.

'I'll give him Angus's address,' Kate
said, 'and ask him.'

Caroline's eyes still brimmed with
laughter. Kate was such an honest girl

. . . not like Sally.

Her eyes sobered for a moment as she thought of the youngest girl. Sally was going to be a handful.

The last time Caroline had called, the girl had been full of the new assistant manager at the hotel. What was his name again? David Martin, she remembered.

Sally was very keen to have the reception at the hotel, and for David Martin to be invited to the wedding as a guest. Oh well, pretty girls like Sally were bound to find a number of boyfriends before they settled down.

Caroline's thoughts went to Keith. If he had been as fun loving as Sally, she might have understood his sudden visit to London, but Keith was rather the opposite. He only seemed to have time for his job, then a quiet evening at home.

★   ★   ★

Gavin Reid and Keith arrived a short time later, still talking about the relative merits of a new treatment for preserving wood.

Gavin Reid was a little quieter than usual as he looked at Keith. One of their best men had recently left to go abroad, and Keith hadn't been too happy about losing him.

Had the boy got someone in mind for the job, when he was going off to London at the drop of a hat?

Surely if he wanted a change, and a rest, he wouldn't have chosen London! He had mentioned this to Sally, who had laughed at him.

'Oh, Dad, you are silly,' she said. 'In fact, Keith Drummond rises in my estimation. London will do him the world of good, you'll see.'

That settled it in Gavin Reid's mind, and they left the workroom in the care of one of the other men.

It could all jog along now until after the wedding, Gavin Reid thought, but perhaps he should think about taking up the reins again in a small way.

Kate managed a word with her future

stepbrother after Mrs Simpson had gone, and she slipped Angus's address into his hand. Keith looked at it, a strange expression on his face.

'Try to see Angus for me?' she asked him. 'I think he should be at the wedding, don't you?'

'Er . . . of course,' Keith said rather awkwardly.

Kate's days were taken up with choosing something pretty to wear for the wedding, her choice going to a lovely silk dress and coat.

Sally looked at it half-enviously. For the most part she was entirely satisfied with her own looks, but there were times when she thought that Kate had a style and elegance she could never achieve.

'Lovely,' said Sally. 'I wish I hadn't chosen that shade of pink now. It's sugary.'

'It makes you look very sweet,' said Kate.

'I know . . . sugary,' Sally repeated. 'I think that shade of clover pink is wrong for Gemma. It make her look too pale.'

'Yes, she is pale,' Kate said, reflectively. 'No wonder, with Norrie to look after. Anyway, his father will keep him in order at the wedding. Alec never stands for any nonsense.'

She removed her dress and jacket, hanging them away, and then went to answer a knock at the door. It would be another present, most likely. Her father was a very popular man.

It was Angus Fraser.

Kate took one look at him, and her face lit up with joy.

'Angus! So you've come home!'

'Hello, Kate,' he said, smiling, his hazel eyes almost green with excitement as they took stock of one another.

Kate hugged him for joy, then stepped back as Mr Reid and Sally arrived, startled by the sound of his deep rich voice.

'Come in,' Gavin Reid invited. 'My word, Angus, but you've grown. No, I don't mean that. I mean . . . er . . . '

'That I've aged a lot?' Angus asked,

laughing. 'Just look at this child, too!'

'Child!' Sally cried. 'I'm a reception-ist at the hotel, in case you've forgotten!'

'Sorry, sorry.'

Angus followed the girls into the sitting-room.

Kate hardly knew whether she was standing on her head or her heels. The Frasers would be so happy to have Angus home, especially Lachie.

'Tell us all about London,' she said.

'She always wants to hear every-thing,' Sally interrupted, 'every little detail, but this time I'm listening, too. It must be wonderful to live in London.'

'It's been . . . quite an experience,' Angus said slowly.

He turned to Mr Reid, who was looking at Angus with pride. The boy was mature now, well balanced and capable.

'Do you think we could have a little talk later, Mr Reid?' he asked.

'Certainly,' Gavin Reid told him.

'We'll go and make supper,' said

Kate. 'Come on, Sally.'

Sally went with her reluctantly. For once she wanted to be in on Angus Fraser's conversation, and hear about London.

Not that Stronmore was without its attractions at the moment. David Martin, the new assistant manager at the hotel, was a very exciting man. He wasn't at all like the usual dull types she usually met.

When Kate finally carried a tray through, her father and Angus were both very quiet, as they sat looking into the fire.

Yet Mr Reid had an air of relief and genuine delight which he found increasingly difficult to hide. Finally he turned to Kate.

'Angus is coming back to Stronmore,' he said, 'to work in the firm. He's leaving London.'

Angus bit his lip.

'You might as well know, Kate. I . . . I haven't quite made the grade. You've got to be very talented, and very special, to make a living in fine art. Very lucky, too,' he added half to himself.

'Oh, Angus,' Kate said softly.

She looked at him, and for a long moment it was as though they could see into each other's souls, and she was strongly aware of his inner torment. Then the moment had gone, and Angus was smiling happily.

'I'll be glad to be back. There's nowhere like Stronmore.'

'You're a fool,' Sally said, and for once her father turned on her.

'That's enough, Sally!' he cried.

\* \* \*

Angus's arrival just seemed to put the final touch on the wedding arrangements, and Kate glowed when the day arrived.

The wedding was a lovely, simple ceremony, and Caroline looked beautiful. Gavin Reid was at his best, and even Keith seemed to have shed his worries as he smiled happily at everyone. His holiday had done him all the good in the world.

Lachie Fraser had hardly been able to keep his eyes off Kate, and the news that Angus was coming back home again was giving him pause for deep thought.

Kate and he had been very close over these past few months. He had known she would not think about her own future while her father needed her, but things were different now, surely.

After an excellent meal at the hotel a small four-piece band arrived and soon the place was full of dance music.

Lachie rose to his feet and claimed Kate for a waltz, then waltzed her out through the french windows, to the cool peace of the lovely Stronmore Castle gardens.

As they stopped dancing, Kate took his arm companionably and they walked slowly along the grass verge.

'Oh, Lachie.' She sighed. 'Hasn't it all gone well? It's funny how you worry about things ... even little things

. . . then they all seem to disappear into nothing at a time like this. I suppose that's because everyone is happy.'

'I know what you mean, Kate,' he told her seriously.

They were silent for a while, listening to the faint sounds of music from the hotel.

'This is going to make quite a difference to you, isn't it, Kate?' Lachie asked.

'In what way?'

'Oh, you know, not having your father to look after, and all that.'

'I've still got my job, Lachie.'

'Oh, yes, but you must be feeling that you're free now.'

She looked at him doubtfully.

'You mean, you think that Father and Caroline . . . ?'

'No, it has nothing to do with your father and Caroline,' he interrupted her. 'It's to do with us.'

'Kate, I've got to tell you — I've been keeping it to myself for so long — I want to marry you, Kate. I've been in love with you for ages. I think you feel the same way about me . . . '

Kate stared at him, the blood slowly leaving her face with shock. What was Lachie saying? That he wanted to marry her! But she had never thought about marriage in connection with Lachie.

No, that wasn't quite true, she thought honestly. She had sometimes wondered, especially when Angus went away. But now Angus was back . . .

'Oh, Lachie,' she said in a whisper. 'No, don't ask me to marry you. I . . . I can't marry you.'

He stared at her, disappointment in his eyes. He had left it too late.

'It's Angus, isn't it?' he asked, bitterness welling up inside him. 'It's because of Angus. That's it, Kate, isn't it?'

'Leave me alone,' she cried, pulling away. How could Lachie spoil things like this!

He stared at her, then turned away, and Kate was left alone, shivering with nerves and upset. Somehow she felt that things would never be the same again.

She turned away, looking up suddenly to find Angus by her side. For a long moment he stared at the tears on her cheeks, then he put an arm round her shoulders.

'What's wrong, Kate?' Angus asked, 'What's happened?'

# Before They Came Home

Kate stared at Angus, hardly seeing him for a moment, then her face flushed with embarrassment and she pushed him away.

'Tell me, Kate. What's upsetting you?'

'I . . . I don't know what you mean, Angus,' she said unsteadily.

'You're crying. I can see you've been upset . . . '

'Oh, don't be silly, Angus,' she said, trying to laugh it off. 'We're at a wedding, remember? Now you'll have to excuse me, I want to have a word with Gemma.'

Slowly Angus removed his hand from her shoulder, not at all satisfied with Kate's explanation.

He could always tell when she was trying to put him off. She and Lachie had been in deep conversation when he first spotted them, and now he wondered what Lachie had been saying to her.

'Was it Lachie?' he asked abruptly. 'Was he upsetting you?'

'I . . . I've told you, it's nothing,' Kate said almost brusquely, and turned away from him towards the hotel lounge.

Angus looked after her standing still and quiet for a long time. Kate had grown up quite a lot while he was away, but the years had only added to her beauty and personality.

He had met a number of girls with whom he had become quite friendly while on his art course, but none of them could match Kate Reid.

He sighed and turned back towards the garden, then paused once again. Lachie was standing in the shadows, watching him intently.

Angus wanted to go and sort it out with his brother, but something in Lachie's attitude made him pause, and they stared at one another for a long moment.

Angus knew he could forgive his young brother anything, but he wouldn't have him upsetting Kate.

Suddenly Lachie slipped back into the shadow of the trees and was gone. Slowly and thoughtfully he, too, went back into the lounge of the hotel.

Kate walked through the lounge, wishing she could erase all traces of tears from her eyes.

Gemma had wanted a word with her, and Kate deliberately put Lachie to the back of her mind. She would worry about him later.

In the meantime, it was her own family who needed her attention, and Gemma hadn't been her usual happy self for some weeks.

She looked around for Sally, seeing that she was dancing with David Martin, the assistant manager of the hotel.

One or two friends called out a greeting and Kate stopped to speak with them, then she saw Gemma with her husband, Alec, in a corner of the lounge.

Little Norman had had a big day, but now lay against his father's shoulder, crying a little fretfully.

He really was at a difficult age, thought Kate, as she moved forward towards them, then she paused as she saw Gemma and Alec were having an argument.

'What chance have we got to have a break?' Gemma was saying. 'You just don't see anything, Alec . . . '

'I'm thinking of the future,' Alec said, 'not just the present.'

'But it's the present we live in, Alec,' Gemma said. 'There might well be gold across the desert, but we can die of thirst trying to reach it. We'll have to take Norrie home now.'

'He needs more discipline!'

'He needs love.'

'Do you think I don't love my own son?'

They had always been so happy in their marriage, and so proud of their baby son. It made Kate wonder what pressures they were under to make them at odds with one another.

Suddenly she heard her name called as Gemma spotted her, and she turned back again towards them.

'I . . . I came to see if I could help with Norman,' she said huskily.

Gemma's cheeks were rose pink, and her eyes shone brilliantly.

'We're going home,' Gemma said. 'Norrie is tired.'

'Oh, but surely I could look after him for you,' Kate suggested. 'Then you and Alec could dance together.'

'Oh. Alec has too much to do at home to waste his time dancing,' Gemma replied tersely.

Alec turned and smiled at Kate.

'It's nice of you to offer,' he said gently, 'but I think the excitement has tired all of us. As Gemma says, we'll just slip away now.'

Suddenly the microphone crackled, and David Martin's voice came clearly making the announcement that the bride and groom were now leaving.

'I'd better go and wish them well.'

Kate turned to go.

'We'll all go,' Alec said, while Norman clung round his neck. 'This chap can wait for five minutes for such a special occasion. It isn't all that long past his bedtime. Come on, darling, let's see them off.'

He sounded much more like the old Alec, thought Kate, but now that the anger had left Gemma, she saw how very tired her older sister looked.

\* \* \*

Gavin Reid and the new Mrs Reid looked very happy and excited as they tried to avoid showers of confetti amidst a great deal of laughter.

Caroline had never looked more lovely, thought Kate, as her new stepmother paused to receive the good wishes of their many friends.

Kate slipped through a group of the guests to reach her father's side, delighted to see how fit and well he looked.

Caroline turned to see her husband holding his daughter's hands, then Kate turned to her, kissing her on the cheek.

'Be happy, Caroline,' she said simply.

'Thank you, darling . . . '

Caroline paused as she saw the luminous look in Kate's eyes. The girl had been crying, and it had been the hot tears of anxiety, rather than bright tears of happiness.

'Are you all right, Kate?' she whispered urgently.

'Oh . . . everything's fine,' said Kate brightly.

She avoided Caroline's eyes, though her face flushed, having caught sight of Lachie at the back of the crowd. She wanted time to herself before she talked to him again.

'Don't do too much, then,' Caroline warned, laughter in her voice. 'I can soon take care to things when I . . . when we get back home.'

Caroline turned away to find Keith by her side, though her thoughts were still on Kate.

She always believed she knew Kate well, as though she were indeed her own daughter. Yet the girl had been reserved with her, and was obviously upset now that the wedding was all over.

Could it be that, deep down, Kate still remembered her own mother? Was she trying her best to accept, and even love, a stepmother, but hadn't been able to keep her true feelings hidden until the wedding was all over?

Caroline accepted the other good wishes brightly, pausing with Gavin for photographs, but her eyes were on Kate's small, expressive face.

No, something was troubling the girl, she thought. However, she wouldn't allow it to interfere with Gavin's and her own happiness — at least until they returned home again.

'Kate looks tired,' she said, turning to Keith. 'See that she gets home all right, won't you, dear?'

'So you've got more than one chick to worry about now, Mother!' Keith teased her, and Caroline laughed.

Then she and Gavin were in the car, waving to their guests. Kate watched them go, and turned to find Keith by her side.

'Come on, sister Kate,' he said. 'I'll see you home, unless you want to stay for another dance or two.'

'No, I'll be glad to get home,' she said sincerely.

At least she would be spared having to refuse either Lachie or Angus. They were no longer children together, she thought rather sadly. Now things had changed between the three of them.

★　★　★

In spite of what Caroline had said, Kate decided that Hazelbank was going to be as bright and fresh as she could make it, before her father and Caroline came back from their honeymoon.

She was beginning to recover from the upsetting part of the wedding, and put it into its true perspective.

People always became emotionally involved at a wedding — even so she would allow Lachie a few days before seeing very much of him again. He had been angered by her refusal, and would need time to get over it.

'The larder is a bit dingy,' she said to Mrs Simpson, after they had cleared everything off the shelves. 'I think I'll buy a pot of white paint and brighten it up.'

'You'll work yourself to a standstill,' Mrs Simpson grumbled. 'And you'll have everything smelling of paint.'

'That's why I'm going to do it straightaway and give it time to dry properly before Father and Caroline come home.'

'You wouldn't like my Bob to come along and fix up new shelves while you're about it?' Molly Simpson asked her.

'No, thanks all the same. I think these ones are OK. Besides, your husband must be busy in the workshop.'

'He is,' Mrs Simpson agreed. 'The

men are all really pleased to see Angus back. Keith is a fine young man, but they always say two heads are better than one. They seem to be able to get everything going much better between them, or so Bob says.'

'Oh, that's fine.' Kate was aware of her feelings rising at the mention of Angus. It was good to have him home, she acknowledged to herself.

Yet was she glad that Angus had returned home permanently?

She had been happy for a while with Lachie's warm friendship and might even have thought seriously about his proposal. But Angus's return had confused her.

Lachie was right when he had accused her of turning him down because of Angus. Not because she was sure of her feelings, but rather because she was so very unsure.

Until Caroline came along, Kate had always put her own affairs to the back of her mind, believing she must put her family first.

Before Angus had gone away things might have been resolved between them but for those responsibilities.

There had been something on Angus's mind then, too, she thought shrewdly.

He had felt that he must succeed, not only for himself, but . . . for whom? Could she have been his other reason?

He had felt compelled to justify the step he had taken, perhaps to show the people who had had faith in him that it wasn't misplaced.

Yet now he had returned, and had admitted to her father that he'd failed. Wouldn't that failure be hurting Angus underneath?

As Kate painted the larder, her thoughts kept her mind occupied. Her feelings and sympathies going to Angus, then to Lachie, whose hopes must have taken a setback, then back to Angus again.

She was so glad the men were happy to have him back. Surely that must go a long way to balancing his failure in London.

Her father had often said that Angus had a real feeling for old furniture and could tell if a piece was worth restoring just by giving it a quick look over.

At that moment, Angus's hazel eyes were clouded a little as he went over the firm's books with Keith.

'Well, things could be a little better, Keith,' he said quietly, 'but we'll leave this aside for the moment. What was it you were worried about?'

'Old Mrs Clark's cottage. She lives next door to Bob Simpson, but she needs a wee bit of repair work done in her living-room. I've given her an estimate and it should all be plain sailing, but we've been a bit slow in getting round to it. Maybe we could spare Bob Simpson next week . . . '

'Hmmm.'

Angus looked at the work schedule. It was difficult to assess just how long the repairs would take since most of them were for highly-specialised work.

However, Mr Reid always liked to accommodate local people who needed small repairs done.

'I've got one of our young apprentices along there now,' Keith said, 'preparing the work for Bob.'

'We'll call in and take a look on the way home.' Angus decided. 'It would be as well to have Mrs Clark's repairs finished before we take on Tordale Parish Church. We'll need to renew some panelling and it won't be an easy job.'

Old Mrs Clark was delighted to see Angus and Keith.

'You'll have a cup of tea?' she asked, not taking no for an answer. 'Sit down. Mr Drummond, and you, Angus . . . er . . . Mr Fraser . . . '

'Angus.' He grinned, assuring her that he would welcome some tea, then he walked over to the side of the room near the window where the plaster had crumbled.

It had all been cleaned away, and everything tidied, but for a long moment Angus stared at the wooden beams, testing the wall in various places.

Mrs Clark had hurried into her kitchen and Angus called Keith over.

'Have a look at this, Keith,' he said and began to explain the probable structure of the wall. 'Now, you see how this beam makes the main support.'

'Yes,' Keith said. 'What about it, Angus?'

'Can't you see? It's got dry rot.' Angus said quietly. 'The whole of that wall will have to come down, to get at the root of the trouble. It isn't a case of doing a simple repair. It's going to be a major one, instead.'

'Oh dear,' Keith said. 'I've only estimated for a few hours' work. It'll cost far more than that.'

⋆   ⋆   ⋆

There was a sound of breaking crockery behind them, and both young men whirled round to see old Mrs Clark staring at them, her plate of biscuits on the floor.

'Did . . . did you say it was going to

cost an awful lot?' she asked, her voice trembling. 'Oh dear, Angus. Is it really a big job? I haven't enough money for that.'

'Now, just you sit down.' Angus told her, pulling forward a chair, even as Keith bent down to pick up the biscuits.

'I'll get you some more,' she said.

Keith was looking at Angus anxiously. He had been making too many mistakes like this, estimating for a job which looked simple and quick, but which proved to be far from simple once they'd started to do it.

How could he have put such an added burden on to them, over Mrs Clark's repairs? Yet it was obvious the old woman couldn't afford the sort of bill which would make the job economical.

'If we don't take the wall down, it could be very serious indeed, Mrs Clark,' Angus was telling her, 'so I'm afraid it will have to be done.'

'I haven't enough put by,' Mrs Clark

told him. 'We got through our savings when John was so ill. I . . . I don't know what to do, Angus.'

Angus glanced at Keith and for a while there was silence while Mrs Clark poured out their tea, then went through to the kitchen for more hot water, her gentle face white and strained.

'I feel awful, Angus,' Keith whispered.

'Me, too,' said Angus. 'But I've been thinking. Now that I'm home, I've got plenty of time in the evenings. I could do it for Mrs Clark in my own time and it wouldn't cost her a penny extra.'

Mrs Clark returned, and both young men turned to her, while Angus explained their solution to the problem.

'Oh, I couldn't do that!' she said, sitting down abruptly.

'Leave it to me, Mrs Clark.'

The old woman stared at him, pressing her lips together as she fumbled in her pocket for a handkerchief.

'I don't know what to say,' she told him.

'Say nothing. I'll be along as soon as I can to investigate the root of the trouble. Don't worry, Mrs Clark, we can't have your house falling down around your ears.'

Mrs Clark watched them go, her heart too full for words. Keith, too, was silent for a while as they walked along together.

'I don't know what to say, either, Angus,' he admitted.

Angus shrugged. 'We're both in this together. Keith and you wouldn't believe the mistakes I made before I went to London.

'But it's all experience and we're learning from it whether we realise it or not. We'll have to learn to look at things from every angle.'

'But you've let yourself in for a great deal of work.'

Angus's eyes sobered. He'd had plans for using his time off, but now they would have to be shelved for a little while.

'It'll soon be finished, Keith, and forgotten.'

'It won't be forgotten,' said Keith quietly.

If he ever assessed anything again, he would just remember Angus having to work on Mrs Clark's cottage!

'Are you coming in for a word with Kate and Sally?' Keith asked as they approached Hazelbank.

Angus hesitated. He hadn't seen Kate since the wedding, nor had he yet been able to have a word with Lachie, who seemed to be very busy from morning till night.

Perhaps he ought to wait a little before he saw Kate again. She hadn't been exactly eager to talk to him before! Slowly he shook his head.

'No, I'll just get along home now, Keith.'

'See you in the morning then, Angus.'

From the window Kate watched Angus turning away from the gate, and her eyes sobered. In the old days he would never have passed without taking a quick look in to see them all.

Perhaps he'd been hurt when she refused to talk to him at the wedding. Kate bit her lip. She hadn't intended to hurt Angus.

She had only felt she couldn't talk to him freely, but how could she explain that to him?

★   ★   ★

Over the next week, Kate found she was tending to avoid Lachie. After a day or two he began to call as regularly as he had done before, but it was she who was always too busy to go out with him.

'I want everything to be really nice for Caroline,' she explained to him. 'Painting the larder just showed me how shabby other corners have become, so I'm washing down a few walls.'

'You'll do too much.' Lachie said, hardly knowing whether he was being put off, or whether Kate really did need to do all this work. 'Why can't Sally help?'

'Oh, she does,' Kate assured him.

'Does what?' Sally asked brightly, opening the kitchen door.

'Sally is ironing the curtains for me. Aren't you, Sally?' Kate asked, giving her sister a meaningful look.

'Oh . . . am I? Yes, I suppose I am,' Sally agreed, throwing down her handbag. She had been in a cheerful mood since the wedding.

'Well, I'd better go then.' Lachie prepared to leave. 'I'll see you later, Kate.'

'Of course, Lachie.

'You won't always be so busy.

'No.' Kate's cheeks were scarlet. She wasn't used to putting anyone off, and she felt rather at odds with herself.

Sally eyed her slantingly as Lachie swung the gate behind him.

'Poor old Lachie!' she said teasingly. 'His nose is out of joint!'

'What do you mean?' asked Kate.

'Can't hold a candle to his big brother, can he?'

Sally was unprepared for the way Kate took her teasing. Her face went white with anger, and she turned on Sally.

'I don't want to hear any more remarks like that, from you or anyone!' Kate shouted.

'I . . . I didn't mean anything. I was only teasing.'

Kate showed no signs of apologising for her anger.

'Good.' she said crisply. 'I'm glad you're going to iron the curtains, Sally.'

'I hate ironing curtains,' Sally muttered.

'It's the only bit of help you've given.' Kate told her evenly. 'I hope you're going to pull your weight a bit more when Caroline takes over.'

Sally said nothing, though she eyed Kate speculatively. She had her own ideas about what she wanted to do with her life after her father and Caroline came home.

Kate sighed and turned to her sister, smiling apologetically. She could never remain angry for long.

'Sorry, Sally. We can see to the

curtains together. Maybe I have been doing rather too much in the house.'

Kate's head ached a little as she thought about Lachie. He had been her friend all her life, and she hated this present atmosphere between them.

Keith came in a short time later. He had agreed rather quietly to move into big, rambling Hazelbank, and he had chosen two rooms on the top floor which he planned to do up himself.

Sally hadn't gone out of her way to be friendly towards him, so Kate tried to make up for her sister's off-hand manner by fussing over him a little.

'Can I get you something to eat, Keith?' she asked. 'Oh, and Mrs Simpson says if you leave your washing in the kitchen, she will attend to it.'

'That's all right, Kate,' he told her quietly. 'Thank you very much, but I'm used to looking after myself. I'll just go on up if I may. Good night — both of you.'

His smile included Sally, but Kate watched him anxiously. She did hope they would all settle down happily together.

It would spoil things for her father and Caroline if there was any discord, and Keith still walked around the house as though he were treading on eggs. Maybe he would settle down when his mother got home.

'You never know when to leave people alone, do you, Kate?' Sally asked. 'You fuss around him like a mother hen.'

'I'm only trying to make Keith welcome,' Kate pointed out.

Yet she was thoughtful as she walked up to her own bedroom. For once Sally could be right. Perhaps Keith just wanted to be left alone.

The following day was Kate's half day, and she was busily hanging the freshly-ironed curtains when the kitchen door burst open and Norrie rushed in, followed by a rather breathless Gemma.

'He ran like the wind as soon as we got near Stronmore,' she said. 'I couldn't catch up with him, and that main road can be dangerous. Norman, if you slip my hand again . . . '

'I'm a big boy,' he informed them proudly.

'Big boys do what their mothers tell them,' said Kate. 'I'm just finishing, Gemma. Sit down, and we'll have some tea. You look all in.'

'We walked,' Gemma said. 'Alec had to go into Tordale in the car, and he's picking us up on the way home.'

'You shouldn't have walked. I could have come for you. You've really been doing too much.'

'We're short handed,' Gemma said. 'We've lost our student again.'

Kate looked at her sister with concern. Gemma had been flushed with exertion when she walked in, but now she lay back in her chair, her cheeks pale and blue shadows under her eyes.

'I'll put the kettle on,' said Kate, taking Norrie's hand. 'Come on, and we'll look for your favourite biscuits.'

Kate carried the tea-tray back into the living-room while Norman raced around finding the toys always kept for him in the big kitchen cupboard at Hazelbank.

'That should keep him quiet for a little while,' Kate laughed. 'He has obviously been wearing you out, Gemma.'

'Oh, it isn't only Norrie,' Gemma said wearily. 'Kate, I . . . I think I'm having another baby.'

Kate stared for a moment at her sister, then her eyes lit up with delight.

'That's lovely news.'

'It would be, if . . . if only things were better at the farm. Alec does want to make a success of managing Meadowpark for Mr Meldrum. He's got so many new ideas to put into practice which he couldn't use at home because his father and Donald . . . '

'Uncle Donald!' Norman piped up.

Both girls were slightly disconcerted.

'Big-Ears,' whispered Kate, her eyes twinkling.

'Uncle Donald,' Gemma corrected herself. 'They like the old ways best. We're short handed at the moment now that the student has gone, so I've been helping.'

'Oh, Gemma! You shouldn't, not at this stage.'

'But I was fine with Norrie. Never felt better. Only this time I . . . I seem to be tired all the time. And I dread telling Alec. He's got enough on his plate already.'

'Well, drink this cup of tea, anyway, and try to relax a little. You're all strung up.'

Gemma's fingers were trembling as she took the cup, then a moment later she almost dropped it on to the table, the tea spilling into the saucer.

'I . . . I feel a bit giddy,' she said.

Kate pressed her back into her chair.

'Don't move,' she said, looking closely at Gemma's face. 'I'll phone for the doctor straightaway.'

# Break In The Family

For a moment Kate hardly knew which way to turn as she looked anxiously at Gemma. Her sister seemed very white and ill as she lay back in her chair. Kate hurried to the telephone to ring Dr Spiers.

It was Mrs Spiers who answered and as Kate quickly explained the circumstances, her quiet pleasant voice had a calming effect.

'Just allow your sister to rest quietly,' Mrs Spiers said. 'I feel sure I can contact my husband quickly for you.'

'Oh, thanks, Mrs Spiers.' Kate gave a sigh then turned to find an unusually quiet Norman at her elbow, his eyes large and frightened.

'Why won't my mummy play?' he demanded.

'Because your mummy is tired,' Kate answered, putting her arms round him.

His bottom lip stuck out and soon his face crumpled and he began to sob.

'I want my mummy to play. She won't get up.'

'Now be a good boy.' Kate wondered how best to distract him. 'There's your teddy bear who is just every bit as tired as Mummy. You put him to bed with a blanket, while I do the same for Mummy. See who is better at playing nurse.'

Carefully she put a travelling rug round Gemma, having moved her to the settee, while Norrie watched with obvious reluctance, then he joined in the game.

Kate prayed for Dr Spiers to hurry, but it seemed hours before she heard the crunch of his car wheels on the gravel.

A moment later the kindly, elderly doctor was bending over Gemma, while Kate once again had to keep Norrie quiet, and out of the doctor's way.

A new baby in the house would do that young man no harm, she thought, adding a silent prayer that nothing

71

would go wrong for Gemma.

The doctor examined the older girl carefully, then wrapped the travelling rug round her again.

'Well, young Gemma — Mrs Johnstone, I should say — I can't give you a more detailed examination at present, but you've obviously been overdoing things recently, and that hasn't helped your baby any. At this point we can't be too careful. You'll need complete rest for two weeks, at least . . . '

'How can I?' Gemma asked weakly.

Dr Spiers smiled. He'd heard this question asked many times before.

'Ways can be found, my dear. Now I'm going to phone for an ambulance. I'd be happier if you spent the next twenty-four hours in hospital. Just as a precaution,' he added quickly as he saw Gemma's anxious look. 'We'll keep you in for observation.'

At that, he left the room, giving Gemma no time to argue.

★ ★ ★

He found Kate waiting anxiously in the kitchen and quietly explained the situation.

'We'll give her a more thorough examination tomorrow, and decide then what, if anything, has to be done. I must stress that she will need complete rest for at least a fortnight. She shouldn't have been helping with heavy farm work so early in her pregnancy.'

'No,' Kate agreed.

'Will you make my teddy better along with my mummy?' asked Norrie, and the old doctor's eyes crinkled as he took out his stethoscope.

Smiling, Kate watched him examine the teddy bear, again with great care, and pronounce that he'd soon be better with careful nursing.

A few minutes after Dr Spiers had left, Alec's car drew up at the door, and he ran round to the kitchen door.

'Oh, thank goodness you're here, Alec,' Kate greeted him, while Norrie rushed to throw himself into his father's arms.

'What's up?' he asked. 'Has this little fellow been running riot?'

'No, it's . . . '

'My teddy's not well!' Norrie exclaimed in his father's ear.

'It's Gemma,' said Kate.

'Nothing much, Alec,' Gemma called through from the sitting-room.

Tactfully Kate told Alec she would make some tea for everyone.

Alec hurried through to the sitting-room, alarm on his face as he saw how pale his wife was.

Gemma gave him a shaky smile. 'I'm afraid I've given everyone a bit of a fright. Sorry.'

Alec looked puzzled. 'But what happened?'

Gemma hesitated. 'I felt a bit faint, that's all. It's nothing to worry about, but I'll need to take things easy for a little while — until the baby is born.'

She looked anxiously at Alec as he took in what she had just said.

'The baby,' he repeated. 'You mean . . . ?'

'Yes. I'm expecting another baby.'

'Why didn't you tell me?' Alec asked her. 'You shouldn't have been helping out on the farm. If only I'd known . . . '

'I couldn't tell you until I knew for sure. Besides,' Gemma's voice grew more serious, 'you've had enough worries recently. And now I've gone and added to them. Dr Spiers said I'll need to go into hospital overnight and then take things easy for the next few weeks.'

'Dr Spiers said complete rest,' Kate interrupted as she came into the room carrying a tray. 'You could come and stay here once you leave the hospital.'

'It would be upsetting for Norrie,' Gemma protested, while Alec looked half anxious and half proud.

'I'll rest at home. That way I can supervise all that has to be done.'

'But you won't rest,' Kate said, knowing her sister. 'I'll have to come and stay at the farm for a few days at least.'

'But you're needed here . . . ' Gemma began half-heartedly.

'Sally will just have to look after Hazelbank for now.'

'Fat chance!'

'Oh, she might surprise us both one of these days. She has some holidays due. I'm sure she could take them now.'

They were interrupted by a ring at the doorbell. It was the ambulance for Gemma. Kate hurriedly packed some things for her to use until Alec could bring her own things from the farm.

At Gemma's insistence. Alec didn't accompany her to the hospital but set off for the farm with a rather tearful Norman in tow.

'I'll be with you as soon as I can, Alec,' Kate told him.

'Bless you,' he said huskily, and turned to wave at the ambulance, while Norrie raced to the car, his teddy bear trailing on the ground.

Kate watched them go, then turned to the telephone. Sally would have to come home, whether she wanted to or not.

The hotel didn't appear to be too well organised when Kate rang up. The telephone was allowed to ring for some time, then a girl answered, asking her to hold on for a moment. Finally she was told that Sally was no longer employed in reception.

'Then where is she?' Kate asked.

'I'm sorry, madam, I don't know,' she was told.

'You mean she isn't in the hotel now?'

'Oh, no, madam. As I told you, she's no longer employed here.'

Kate put down the telephone weakly. What did they mean, that Sally had left her job? If she wasn't at the hotel, then where was she?

She had left for work as usual that morning . . . no, she had left early, Kate remembered, and she had been in a rather restless, uncertain mood the previous evening.

Kate hurried up to Sally's room, her

mouth dry with apprehension.

Where had Sally gone? Were her clothes still in the wardrobe?

Opening the wardrobe door, Kate was relieved to see several things hanging up, but a moment later she saw that a great many had gone.

The dressing-table, too, was much tidier than usual.

Then Kate saw that a pale lilac-coloured envelope had been propped up against the mirror. With trembling fingers she opened the envelope and took out the letter.

*I know you'll just argue if I tell you,* Sally had written, *and I want to live my own life. David Martin has found me a super job in London, and I've got a room . . .*

Slowly Kate read on, feeling sick and shaken. How far apart she and Sally were growing, when her young sister couldn't confide in her.

Yet, she was quite right. Kate would have tried to talk Sally out of it. She was so young to take a step like this.

And at such a time, just when Gemma so badly needed the help of the rest of them.

Kate wanted to lie on the bed and have a good cry, but she knew that would be of no use to anyone. If only she had someone to turn to!

Suddenly her thoughts went to Angus, who would no doubt be busy over in the workshop. A moment later she snatched up her cardigan, pulling it around her shoulders as she ran out of the back door and round the garden path to the side entrance.

Angus was busy at the work-bench when Kate hurried in.

'Oh . . . you're busy,' Kate began.

'Not too busy to see you.' Angus smiled, noting the look of strain about her eyes. 'What's on your mind, Kate? Come into the office, it's more private.'

'It's Sally . . . and Gemma . . . ' she began once they were out of the workshop, and told him about the need for Gemma to rest.

'I'll have to stay at Meadowpark,' she

said. 'I'd hoped that Sally would help out . . . but she's gone — run away to London! Look. Angus, here's her letter. I . . . I'll have to bring her back. She's far too young to be on her own in London. She didn't tell me about the new job because she knew I'd disapprove — and she was right. It's not for her. I'll have to get in touch with her.'

'Calm down,' Angus said, with his old grin. 'You're a great one for flying off the handle. Just take a deep breath and let's look at this calmly.

'I know you're worried about Sally, but Gemma's your main concern at the moment. Once you've decided how best to help her you can think of Sally.

'She hasn't been completely thoughtless, you know. She's left her address, and at least she has a job and somewhere to stay.

'I know you're upset, Kate. You can't help it, but try not to worry.' Angus gave her an encouraging smile.

'Is there anything I can do? You've only to ask.'

Kate did her best to return his smile. 'Thanks, Angus,' she said. 'I'm sorry to bother you but I just felt I had to tell someone. I'd better get back home now.' She sighed. 'There's quite a lot to do before I go to Meadowpark. I'll have to arrange a few days' holiday.'

Angus watched her go, then sighed as he turned to the paperwork on his desk. He, too, still had a great deal to do.

That evening he was so preoccupied, his mother had to ask him twice if he wanted more tea.

'What? Oh, no, thanks, Mother, this is plenty.'

'Your head is in the clouds,' she said, smiling.

Lachie had just come in and he, too, had joined the family circle round the fireside.

'It's hardly that,' Angus said. 'It's just — well — Gemma Johnstone isn't well. Kate came to see me today, and they're having a hard time at Meadowpark.

'Alec is short handed and Gemma's

81

been helping. Now she has to rest up for a few weeks, or she might lose her baby.'

'You mean she's expecting another baby?'

'That's right,' Angus answered. 'I forgot — few people will know about that yet.'

'I didn't know for one,' Lachie said morosely. 'I'm very sorry for Gemma. She's a nice lass.'

'What are they going to do then?' Mrs Fraser asked.

'Well, she's to stay in hospital overnight and Kate's going to give a hand for a few days at least. I think she's hoping something will turn up.'

'I could perhaps give her a hand,' Mrs Fraser said thoughtfully. 'Or even Molly Simpson. Why doesn't Kate ask her?'

'I'll mention it,' Angus said, nodding. 'Poor girl, she was upset. I don't think she was in any shape to make plans.'

He thought about Kate's problem with Sally, but decided to keep that to himself for the time being.

Kate would want it kept as quiet as possible, at least until her father and stepmother came home.

Lachie watched Angus broodingly, realising Angus was holding something back. So Kate was now confiding in Angus when she was upset! Only a few short weeks ago, she would have been running up the hill to talk to him at the first sight of trouble.

Lachie rose to his feet, looking for his anorak.

'You aren't going out again, are you, Lachie?' Mrs Fraser said. 'You've only just come in.'

'I want a walk to clear my head,' he answered shortly.

Angus looked after him as he strode out of the house. Things were not getting any easier between himself and Lachie.

★   ★   ★

Kate shook her head rather slowly when Angus looked in the following morning on his way to the workshop and repeated his mother's suggestion.

'Then you don't think it's a good idea?' he asked.

'I've already asked Mrs Simpson,' she said gently, 'and she can take over from me at the farm at the end of next week, but only as a temporary measure.

'She can't leave her husband to fend for himself for too long, and it's a fair distance to Meadowpark. She can't travel backwards and forwards for very long.'

'No, I can see that,' Angus mused. 'Oh, there goes Keith on his way to the workshop. I'd better hurry along now, Kate. We . . . we've got rather a lot to see to.'

'Cheerio, and thanks, Angus.'

'No need for thanks. I've done nothing. I haven't forgotten Sally, either. I'll see what can be done.'

Kate watched him go, feeling oddly comforted, then turned to the list she was preparing for Mrs Simpson.

The older woman was excellent at

keeping things clean and tidy, but she never seemed to know how to deal with an emergency.

'That contract from Mr Richmond may be going ahead,' Angus said, excitedly, a few days later as he opened the mail.

'Mr Richmond? You mean for West Lodge?' Keith asked, his eyebrows raised. 'I was beginning to think that was all a myth. I don't think I ever met him.'

'He's one of our keenest fishermen,' Angus laughed. 'Up from London every year and out every day, whether the river is up or not!

'I think he really loves Stronmore and finds it relaxing, standing about in the middle of the river. Though, mind you, he could land a nice fish when the mood was on him.

'My father was his gillie, and he has great admiration for him. He seems to be quite a wealthy man — he's in some sort of metal components.'

'And he actually bought West Lodge?'

'Right. It's in a fine position for the fishing, and he plans to retire there one day. He saw some of the restoration work we've been doing, and he wants us to renovate the lodge.

'It was put off for a while when Mr Richmond went abroad. But now he wants us to go ahead with those plans, and if they are approved, he'll sign the contract. One of us must go to London, Keith . . . '

'You go, Angus,' Keith said quickly. 'You know much more about it than I.'

Angus paused. 'That's true, and I'll certainly go — this time. But if something comes up which we both understand, then you'll have to take your turn, Keith. The more experience you can get of all aspects of business, the better, not just for you but for the company, too.'

Keith nodded.

There was no need to say any more. They knew that the West Lodge contract would go a long way towards putting the company back on to its feet.

It was only later that Angus realised how much this London visit might mean to Kate. He could surely spare an hour or two to look up Sally. It might ease Kate's mind about her sister.

On impulse he telephoned home, saying he would be a little late, and drove out to Meadowpark.

Alec Johnstone emerged from the large barn which hummed with machinery, as Angus drove up. He looked tired and rather worn.

'Hello, Angus, nice to see you,' he greeted.

'I've called for a word with Kate,' Angus said, nodding. 'I don't want to keep you back, Alec. I see you're busy. How is Gemma?'

'Looking much better, thank goodness. They've let her come home. Kate's been marvellous.' He pushed back his cap and rubbed his forehead. 'It's been hectic, but we have a new man starting next week which should help.'

Norrie had come out of the house, and now he ran back in, yelling to Kate that they had a visitor. She, too, looked tired when he walked into the big farmhouse kitchen. Gemma was lying on a day-bed beside the window.

'I feel a fraud,' she said to Angus, after he had come to look down at her.

'She has to be shouted at every five minutes,' Kate said, 'or she'd be out of that bed and feeding the young calves. Norrie is helping with that.'

'I'm a big boy,' Norrie said, using his favourite saying.

'I just drove over for a quick word with you Kate,' Angus told her.

'Well, if you come and help me to pen the geese, we can all have supper together. You will stay, won't you, Angus? It's chicken casserole.'

'I certainly won't say no,' he agreed.

★   ★   ★

Outside he told Kate about his visit to London, his excitement over the contract evident.

'It means a lot, doesn't it?' Kate asked.

'It sure does,' Angus said fervently, then felt he could have bitten out his tongue. 'Er . . . well . . . any contract is important, Kate. You must know that.'

'Yes, I know that, but I've also watched you and Keith over these past few weeks, and you've been running around like scalded cats. I've seen you both looking very anxious, Angus. When my father gets home . . . '

'No,' Angus said sternly, 'You're letting your imagination run on, Kate. It isn't that bad. Just let Keith and me sort it all out. Things fluctuate in business.'

They stared at one another, and finally Kate nodded. She was being told to mind her own business.

'And you'll find time to see Sally?' she asked.

'Right. If you give me her address. I'll look her up.'

'I've written to tell her about Gemma,' Kate said. 'She'll just have received the letter today. Maybe . . . maybe she'll decide to come back home.'

Angus said nothing. He didn't think it would be that easy to entice Sally back home unless in direst emergency.

Angus was to leave for London a few days later, after he and Keith had worked long hours perfecting the plans put forward for West Lodge.

'I'm a bit unhappy about this panelling,' Angus had confessed. 'It's very skilled work. It's the sort of thing Tom Andrews tackled before he went abroad. Bob Simpson might be able to manage it, though it would have to be done with great care.'

He thought for a while. 'Perhaps there's no need to worry . . . '

'We need the contract,' Keith said quietly.

'Right,' Angus agreed. 'Let it go as it is.'

'I hope it all goes well,' Keith said, his eyes anxious. 'I'll be interested to hear about it as soon as you get back home.'

'I'm calling on Sally Reid first,' Angus told him, 'to put Kate's mind at rest. Sally went off to London in such a hurry.'

'I know,' Keith said, his face slightly shadowed. He and Sally hadn't really managed to be friends, and now she had moved out of Hazelbank where she had lived all her life.

Keith had tried to intrude as little as possible into the lives of his step-sisters, but although Kate had assured him the old house was now his home, Keith wondered afresh at the wisdom of living at Hazelbank. It might have been better if he had chosen to be independent.

At first the choice had seemed his, alone, to make and he had thought to please his mother and stepfather. But perhaps that decision had been the wrong one for Sally. Had he, perhaps, been responsible for her leaving her home?

Keith worried about this, quietly, and thought he would be as anxious as Kate to know how Sally was faring.

* ★ ★ ★

The interview with Mr Richmond was even more business-like than Angus had imagined.

Clad in his old fishing jacket and hat while on holiday in Stronmore, he had always been genial and easy going, but now he was the crisp businessman who had become wealthy through hard work and making careful decisions.

Now the plans Angus and Keith had drawn up were submitted to careful scrutiny, and Angus found himself answering a great many questions, after which the contract was signed, and it was the more familiar, genial Mr Richmond who stood up with his hand outstretched.

'That seems to be satisfactory, Mr Fraser,' he said. 'Now would you care to join me for dinner?'

Angus hesitated. It was a tempting offer, since he felt it would do no harm to talk to Mr Richmond informally. Then he remembered Kate's small, anxious face, and the short time he had to spare in London.

'I . . . I'm afraid I have other business to attend to,' he began, and Mr Richmond laughed, slapping him on the back.

'I'm sure she is quite charming,' he said, and Angus was disconcerted. Then he smiled and nodded.

'Quite charming,' he agreed, though again his thoughts were on Kate.

The flat Sally shared with two other girls was on the top floor of a block of flats. As he rang the bell, the door suddenly flew open, and a tall girl with fair hair walked out, a coat thrown carelessly over her shoulders.

'Yes?' she asked.

'Sally Reid, please,' Angus said, and the girl looked at him carefully, then smiled.

'I'm June Russell. Sally! A boyfriend for you!'

Angus could hear a faint shriek, and a moment later Sally appeared at the door, her eyes alight with curiosity, though her smile faded a little when she recognised her visitor.

'Angus! What are you doing here?'

A moment later she was looking alarmed.

'Nothing further wrong I hope! Kate wrote to me about Gemma.'

'Nothing more than Kate told you. Can I come in and talk to you?'

'Well, OK, but we are a little untidy.'

The flat was rather more than a little untidy, but Angus noticed it was comfortable.

A third girl, small and plump, was stirring a pan of soup in the tiny kitchen.

'This is Marion,' Sally said carelessly.

'Want some soup?' she asked.

Angus sniffed appreciatively, and accepted.

'You worried Kate quite a bit,' he told Sally quietly.

'Oh, now, if you've come to talk me into coming back home, then you'll be blue in the face,' Sally said. 'I was bored stiff at home in Stronmore. It's great here in London, I love my job, and . . . and the flat, and the girls. For the first time in my life, I'm doing what I want, and you — '

'I haven't,' Angus interrupted mildly.

'You haven't come to persuade me to come home?'

'No. You're old enough and responsible enough to look after yourself. You come from that sort of a family. I only came to wish you luck in your new job. I'm sure Kate will be pleased to hear you're happy in London, and have made nice friends.'

Marion smiled at him as she handed him a bowl of hot soup.

'I'm the cook,' she said. 'Sally does our hair, and June knows all about clothes.'

'It sounds like an excellent arrangement,' Angus said.

'I also look after the bills and things,' June added. 'Which reminds me, the landlord will be knocking any time now, so rent money please, girls.'

'Oh, I'd forgotten that you'd want

'money today.' Sally frowned and reached out for her handbag.

Angus watched her as she fished out her purse and counted out the notes.

She gave a sigh and started counting out what she had left.

'Have you enough money?' Angus asked her quietly.

She glared at him. 'Yes, thank you,' and tossed her head defiantly. 'Don't worry about me, I've told you I can manage. Besides, I get paid tomorrow so I only need bus fares.'

'Have you nothing left for emergencies?' Angus frowned as he spoke.

Sally laughed lightly. 'What emergencies? Honestly, Angus, you're as big a fusspot as Kate.'

Angus was growing impatient with Sally.

'Kate's only concerned about you — you shouldn't laugh at her like that.'

'Oh, Angus, why so serious? You know I don't really mean it!'

'All the same,' he added, 'it would be

nice if you could appreciate all Kate does for you.'

Sally said nothing more but looked down, studiously gazing at the floor.

'Thank her for me, will you?'

'Of course,' Angus assured her. 'Now, I must hurry. I've a sleeper to catch.'

'I'll see you to the door,' Sally told him.

As he reached the door, Angus had one last try.

'Sally, you are quite sure you want to stay, aren't you?' he asked.

Once again Sally's blonde head lifted defiantly.

'Yes, Angus. I'm sure. This is what I want to do — I've got to prove I can manage on my own — and I will.'

Angus smiled. 'I rather think you will, Sally. But don't forget we're all there if you need us.'

'Thanks, Angus. I won't. You — you'd better hurry, it's getting late.'

Angus noticed the tears in Sally's eyes. He bent down and kissed her lightly on the forehead.

'Look after yourself,' he murmured and left.

★ ★ ★

The following Sunday Mr and Mrs Reid returned home from their honeymoon in France to a much quieter house than they had anticipated.

Kate had intended to return home, since Mrs Simpson would be going over to Meadowpark on Monday, but the older woman had developed a bad cold, and Kate had been forced to ask for another week's leave from her job.

'I can't go taking this cold to your sister and the wee boy,' Mrs Simpson had said dismally. 'She's got enough to worry about already, and it might put the child into his bed.'

'That would be all we need!' Kate agreed fervently.

'No, you stay at home, Mrs Simpson. We'll manage for a few more days.'

Angus had called to see her, and set her mind at rest about Sally.

'She's in love with all the excitement,' Angus said. 'I know how she feels, but maybe she'll decide to stay on, or maybe she'll come home some time. Who knows? She'll just have to find her own feet.'

'You decided to come home, Angus,' Kate remarked, and Angus looked startled then turned away, avoiding her eyes.

'Yes,' he said, briefly. 'I decided to come home.'

Kate bit her lip. Was Angus regretting that decision already? Had his visit to London unsettled him, she wondered.

'Father and Caroline are due home on Sunday,' she said, changing the subject.

'They'll find everything in good shape, I'm quite sure,' Angus said comfortingly. 'You've done a wonderful job.'

'I don't want Father to be worried about Gemma — or Sally — or anything else — '

'He won't. They're both fine. Don't

worry so much, Kate.'

He squeezed her hand, and she laughed ruefully.

'I'm like an old mother hen, I suppose.'

'I wouldn't describe you as an old hen,' Angus told her, his eyes crinkling as he looked at her small face.

'I'll go back home for a few hours on Sunday,' she said. 'Just to prepare things for Father and Caroline.'

Although Kate tried hard to be on time, there was only Keith at home to meet his mother and Gavin Reid as they walked in the door, their faces glowing with happiness.

'Welcome home,' Keith said. 'It's great to see you both looking so well.'

'Hello, Keith,' Gavin greeted him, while Caroline hugged her tall, handsome son.

'Where are the girls?' Gavin asked.

'Er . . . Kate is over seeing to Gemma — she's been a bit off colour. She should be here soon.'

'Not well?' asked Gavin.

'Oh, the crisis is past, and Kate will want to tell you about it,' Keith said quickly.

'And Sally?' Caroline Reid asked.

Keith avoided her eyes.

'Er . . . she's got another job,' he said. 'She — she's gone to London.'

'London!' Gavin exclaimed.

Caroline Reid saw Keith turn away, and knew he didn't want to discuss this. Why had Sally left so hurriedly, she wondered.

Had she been determined to leave the house before her stepmother arrived home?

Some of Caroline Reid's new happiness and excitement ebbed away. Her new life at Hazelbank was not going to be quite as wonderful as she had hoped.

# Keeping The Secret

Kate Reid could see her father's car parked outside the front door at Hazelbank, as she hurried home from Meadowpark Farm, and her heart pounded with a mixture of joy and disappointment.

It was wonderful to have her father and Caroline home again, but she'd had plans for a 'Welcome Home Party,' and now everything seemed to have gone wrong.

Caroline had seen her from the window, and as Kate swung in the gate the front door flew open and suddenly nothing seemed to matter any more, as she hugged her stepmother and her father.

Gavin Reid looked better than he had done for years, his face bronzed by the sun.

'Well, you've certainly been taking

good care of Father already, Caroline.' Kate laughed. 'In fact, he looks far too young to be my father!'

'And I feel too old to have this new bride for a mother,' Keith said, his eyes twinkling with fun.

Glancing at him, Kate suddenly realised how lonely Keith must have felt at times, while his mother was away.

'I understand Sally has left home,' Caroline said.

'She just wants to spread her wings,' Kate told her quickly. 'The real news is about Gemma. She's expecting a baby.'

Gavin Reid had been frowning over the news of his youngest daughter, but now his eyes lit up. He loved children and went a long way towards spoiling Norrie who could get almost anything out of his grandfather. Now the news about another baby in the family was a real delight.

'That's wonderful news!' he cried. 'Isn't it, darling?'

Caroline Reid was looking very

preoccupied. Her thoughts very much on Sally.

'What?' she asked.

'Gemma is expecting another baby.'

'Why, that is wonderful!' Caroline exclaimed. 'Of course it's good news.'

Kate was looking at her closely. She had expected a more spontaneous delight from Caroline and in an odd sort of way, she was disappointed. Surely Caroline would want to become involved in the affairs of the family, especially the ones which brought happiness into their lives?

'I'll go and get tea,' she said, and Caroline rose from the chair.

'I'll help you, Kate.'

'Oh no, not this time. You've had a long journey home. You're off the hook for this evening.'

Caroline Reid hesitated, then sat down again. Perhaps it wouldn't be easy for Kate to hand over the reins, but if Hazelbank was to become her home, she would have to run it.

She stared at the leaping flames of

the fire, while Gavin and Keith talked, and thought about the life which lay ahead. She must somehow carve out her own niche in Hazelbank.

Over tea, Kate asked Caroline about the honeymoon trip which had taken them to France.

'How far did you get?' she asked.

'Oh, we ended up in the Dordogne area, not too far from Bordeaux,' her stepmother replied, smiling with pleasure at the recollection of a happy trip.

'We travelled south through Le Mans and Poitiers, and we spent some time at Bergerac, where Cyrano de Bergerac lived, and we had a lovely time exploring a great many old castles. We've got slides and photographs to show you.'

'Let's have a real family get-together,' Kate suggested. 'Just as soon as Gemma is feeling a bit stronger, then we can all see your souvenirs. Perhaps Sally will find time to come home one weekend, too.'

'There was no need for her to rush

off like that, was there?' Gavin asked rather angrily.

'She's just doing her own thing' Kate told him quickly, and then there was an awkward silence.

'Mrs Simpson has a cold,' Kate continued, changing the subject. 'I'll pop along to see her after tea. We'll have to manage without her for a day or two, Caroline.'

'I think I'll manage all right, dear,' Caroline said quickly.

Kate nodded. Suddenly she was realising that Hazelbank would be more Caroline's concern than hers from now on. She had known it would, but now the time had come, she felt strangely empty.

'You can run along now if you like,' Caroline Reid was offering. 'I'll do the washing-up.'

'I'll do the washing-up,' Keith interrupted. 'You ladies can just relax, or do whatever you want to do.'

'I knew I'd made a good move acquiring Keith as a son,' Gavin Reid joked — he hated to wash up — and there was ready laughter at the table once more.

Kate excused herself and went to find her anorak.

\*     \*     \*

The Simpson cottage was only a few minutes walk from Hazelbank, but a cold wind had blown up, and Kate pulled the hood of her anorak over her dark hair. She had almost run full-tilt into Lachie Fraser before she saw him, and she pulled up, startled.

'You wouldn't be trying to knock me over, would you?' he asked, and Kate laughed.

'No, Lachie. I'm just going over to see Mrs Simpson, and my head was in the clouds, even if it appeared to be in my anorak! Father and Caroline are back home again, by the way.'

'Is that why your head is in the clouds then?' he asked. 'I would have guessed it was because Angus is back home now. I notice that you and he are as thick as thieves again.'

'Lachie, we've been over all this before . . .'

'Yes, and he's just your good friend, isn't he? The same as always. Yet you run to him as soon as you have any problems to talk over. Not so long ago, you would have asked my advice, Kate. That's so, isn't it?'

Kate's cheeks had flamed. What defence could she put up against the truth? Before Angus came home she would have been running up the hill to the Fraser cottage to ask Lachie for help and advice. She couldn't blame Lachie for being hurt.

'Angus was handy,' she said very gently. 'I was upset over one or two things, and somehow it was quicker to talk to Angus in the workshop, than go running about trying to find you, Lachie. You know that's the truth.'

'It never stopped you before,' Lachie persisted.

Kate sighed. It was no use arguing

with Lachie when he was in a mood, but she hoped he would soon be his amiable self.

They parted company, and Kate walked on feeling rather depressed. She had always been used to treating the Fraser household as an extension of her own home, but could she continue to do so, with Lachie feeling as he did?

A moment later Kate was knocking on Molly Simpson's door, restraining her laughter when she saw that it was Bob who answered.

He wore a pink-flowered apron over his waistcoat, the sleeves of his shirt rolled up to the elbows. He looked at Kate rather sheepishly, then invited her to come in.

Molly was sitting by the fireside, her nose rather red and swollen and her eyes watering.

'I should be OK in a day or two,' she told Kate. 'I'll just have to get better, before Bob burns every pan in the house.'

'Oh, the cheek of it!' Bob said in

mock affront, though his eyes were rueful. 'It's the truth though. You've heard of people who can't even boil an egg. You can add Bob Simpson to the list, or even put him at the top.'

As they chatted, Kate suddenly saw Angus walking up the path of the garden next door, carrying a plank of wood. She gave an exclamation of surprise.

'That's Angus Fraser, isn't it?' she asked.

'It is,' Bob said. 'He . . . he's working at old Mrs Clark's cottage at the moment. If I hadn't been tied up here, I could maybe have given him a hand. Mind you, I tried to offer once before and he would have nothing of it. He says it's his own decision, and he must spend his own time on the job . . . '

'Doing what?' asked Kate.

Bob's face went scarlet when he realised he might have let the cat out of the bag.

'Er . . . he was keeping it quiet,' he said lamely. 'Oh, all right, he is doing some repairs to old Mrs Clark's cottage.'

'At this time of day?' Kate asked. 'He must be putting a lot of his own time into it, surely.'

'Ay, well . . . it's kind of awkward,' Bob told her.

'Apparently Mrs Clark got an estimate for doing repairs to the cottage,' Molly said, coming to his rescue. 'And there was more to it than that. There was dry rot, or something like that.

'At any rate, old Mrs Clark was worried about it, but Angus Fraser set her mind at rest and took the job on himself. He is very good at that sort of thing, is Angus. He's like Bob, too, a real craftsman. Mrs Clark can rest assured that the job will be done properly.'

'I see,' Kate said.

She watched as Angus sawed through the piece of wood swiftly. So Angus had taken on all this extra work just to help old Mrs Clark! How like him to do such a thing.

Kate felt a lump rising in her throat at the thought, though she felt foolish as tears pricked her eyes, trying to keep the sight of them from Molly Simpson's sharp eyes.

'It . . . it's very generous of him,' she said huskily.

'Ay, he's a fine lad,' said Bob Simpson. 'He'll soon have that old body's cottage fit to live in.'

'Yes, I expect he will,' Kate agreed.

★　★　★

The following Saturday morning, the Reid household was unusually quiet, with everyone busy with his or her own thoughts.

Keith had come down rather late for breakfast, finding his mother and Kate still in the kitchen. Gavin wanted a look round the garden to see how his plants were coming along, and shortly afterwards Kate produced a shopping list, deciding she had better go to Tordale before the shops closed.

'Things have become rather disorganised with Molly being away,' she told Caroline. 'But we'd better have these in the house over the weekend. They are basics. We can't really do without salt, can we?'

'Add wholemeal flour and yeast to the list, and I'll bake us some bread,' Caroline told her.

'Mm, home-baked bread,' Kate said, writing the items down. 'I'd love that. Anything else?'

'Not until I've had time to look around,' her stepmother told her.

Caroline watched Kate swinging her basket as she made for her old car, then almost abruptly, she turned to Keith. It was the first time since their honeymoon they had managed a conversation on their own. Keith, she was sure, had been avoiding her.

'I think you'd better tell me what's wrong, Keith,' she said quietly. 'Are you unhappy here at Hazelbank? Is it anything to do with Sally?'

Keith took a gulp of tea.

'Oh, no, it isn't that, Mother,' he said. 'Everything is fine.' His eyes avoided hers.

'Now it's no use pretending with me. I know you too well.'

Keith ran his hand through his hair.

'Well, OK, I'll tell you, but you'd better keep it to yourself for now. It's the business. We ran into a very bad patch just after Mr Reid — Gavin — took ill, and my inexperience didn't help.

'One or two of our best men left, and mistakes were made over costing jobs. That was largely my fault, since I always seem to under-estimate. For a while I thought my wedding present to you both would be a failed company.'

'Keith!'

'Yes, I know,' he said, running a hand through his hair. 'And it isn't over yet, by any means. Angus is working like a slave to help. He's got loads more practical experience than I've got.

'The renovation and reconstruction at West Lodge — Mr Richmond's house

— will help a great deal, but we're not out of the woods yet.

'I'm terrified in case Gavin decides to come in on Monday morning now he's so much better, and wants to see the books. He'll see at a glance that things don't look too good.'

'He mustn't see the books just yet then,' Caroline said quickly. 'I know he looks very well, and very fit, but he still needs building up. Business worries could be a setback.'

Keith nodded. 'That's what I thought,' he agreed. 'But how do we keep him out? The company still belongs to him. We can't keep him out of his own workshop . . . Look out, Mother, he's coming back in.'

'Not another word!' said Caroline, turning to greet her husband with a happy smile. 'Well, darling, has the garden gone back to nature when you weren't around to keep an eye on it?'

'It could do with a wee bit of attention,' Gavin admitted. 'Though it isn't as bad as I had feared. I put in a lot of shrubs and heathers before I took ill, and it's a lot easier to manage. But one or two bushes need careful pruning.'

'I think we could all do with a cup of coffee,' Caroline said. 'There's no rush to do anything, I'm quite sure.'

Her look included Keith, and she saw the lightening in his eyes. He must have been carrying his burden for some time, she thought.

She wished she had noticed how preoccupied he was before the wedding, so she could have helped a little more at that time. She had thought it was because he was coming to terms with the new life which was opening out for both of them, but now she saw it had been much more serious.

Sunday was another quiet day, though Gavin and Caroline went over to Meadowpark in the morning to take some small gifts to Norrie and to see for themselves how well Gemma was keeping. They had now heard all about Gemma's sudden collapse, and were more concerned than they cared to show.

The new man arrived to help Alec — a thin, middle-aged man with greying hair.

Frank Lawson had recently lost his wife, and now he was more anxious to help Alec at Meadowpark, and to be part of their young family even if only as an onlooker.

He had retired quietly into the background after Alec introduced him, but Caroline could see the pleasure in his eyes as he watched young Norrie with his grandfather, both of them entirely satisfied with one another.

Norrie loved the toy car they had brought him from Bordeaux, and wanted to know all about the big boat which had carried his grandfather and his new grandmother across the Channel.

\*   \*   \*

Caroline had time for a quiet word with Gemma.

'I hope you're managing to rest, my dear,' she said. 'It's important for you.'

'I know,' Gemma said ruefully. 'I found that out the hard way!'

'Would it help if I came to stay for a few days?'

'It would be wonderful,' Gemma said, grinning, 'but not at all practical. I think Father will need you at Hazelbank for a little while yet.'

Caroline's eyes darkened. How much did Gemma know? Surely she could not have guessed about the business?

'He won't give you up so easily.' Gemma was laughing now, and Caroline relaxed. The younger girl was now in a teasing mood, she thought, forgetting all her suspicions.

'In any case, Alec's young cousin, Moira, is coming to stay for a week or two. She's young, just nineteen, but she's fond of children and gets on well with Norrie. I'll ring Kate and tell her she can go back to work now. She can drive over and pick up her things.'

'If she can get the car to start,'

Caroline said. 'It was rather temperamental when she took it out this morning.'

'Angus can bring her over, or Lachie,' Gemma decided. 'She'll be glad to get back to her job.'

'Yes,' agreed Caroline. 'Don't hesitate to let us know, Gemma, if you want any help. I'd like to think you could call on me.'

Gemma nodded, and squeezed Caroline's hand.

'I'll let you know,' she promised.

Later, as she stood beside Alec, her heart was more at peace, thanks to her enforced rest.

For a long time she had carried round a constant feeling of irritation, born of her own fatigue, and worry that things weren't going well for Alec. It could be that problems would loom large in the future, but she felt sure she would be more able to cope with them. She slid her hand into Alec's.

'I'm sorry, love,' she whispered.

'What for?' Alec asked, startled.

He turned her round to face him.

'Oh, being bad tempered, and awkward, and wanting to argue all the time.'

'You, bad tempered!' he cried. 'I'm the culprit, darling. Oh, Gemma, I should apologise. I felt I was letting you down.'

'We'll never let one another down, not if we stick together,' Gemma told him. 'It will be hard work with another baby in the house, but we're happy, aren't we?'

'Very happy,' Alec said, contentedly.

'Brrm! Brrm!' said Norrie at their feet, crawling along with his new car.

'Thank goodness for grandparents.' Alec laughed. 'Now, young lady, you must rest.'

Caroline was rather preoccupied again over dinner while Gavin and Keith talked happily together. Kate slanted a glance in her stepmother's direction.

'Should we wash up together, Caroline?' she suggested.

'What? Oh, yes, of course, dear. I think you two men would be more comfortable in the lounge,' she said, 'while Kate and I clear away.'

Kate chose to wash up, and after a moment or two she turned to Caroline.

'You're very quiet today,' she said. 'Are you worried about anything?'

Caroline looked slightly startled, then turned to face Kate honestly.

'Yes,' she said. 'I am. Just a minute.'

She made sure the men were busy, then she shut the kitchen door.

'I've had a talk with Keith, dear, and I'm afraid things haven't been going too well in the business for some time now. I'm worried, because your father's planning to turn up at the workshop in the morning. I don't think he should be faced with business worries just yet, and Keith thinks he and Angus might manage to straighten things out, with hard work, before Gavin finds out.'

She went on to tell Kate what Keith had told her.

'And he kept it to himself!' Kate said

wonderingly. 'Why didn't he tell me — I might have been able to help.'

'Because it was Keith's responsibility, dear. He would never have worried you with it. I'm only telling you now so you can help keep Gavin away. I knew you'd think it odd, if I tried to do it on my own. And I feel that . . . well . . . I don't want you to think it odd, if I tried to do it on my own. I hope you'll explain that to Sally as well. I don't want her to get the wrong idea.'

Caroline looked at her stepdaughter anxiously, but Kate's worries were with her father at the moment, and the business.

'And things haven't been good for some time?' she asked.

'No. A lot of small businesses are having a hard time. It isn't all Keith's fault.'

'I'm sure that none of it is Keith's fault,' Kate said, stoutly. 'And now he's got Angus to help, things should get better.'

'I wonder how we can keep Gavin

away tomorrow.' Caroline sighed. 'Without arousing his suspicion, I mean.'

'We just remind him of his promise to the doctor to stay away, until he is completely fit,' Kate said. 'It's as simple as that. If we are both very firm with him, he'll stay at home. He can't fight both of us.'

'Good girl,' Caroline agreed. 'As you say, the simple truth is always the best.'

\* \* \*

Kate's car had to go in for servicing, but she wanted to go over to see Gemma. She pondered over asking Angus, then remembered he would be busy at Mrs Clark's cottage. Her father and Caroline were going out to friends, and on impulse Kate decided to go and ask Lachie.

'I just want to bring a couple of suitcases and some books from Meadowpark, Lachie,' she said on the telephone. 'The wee pick-up would do.'

'That's OK,' Lachie assured her. 'I'll

be over to fetch you in about half an hour.'

She could tell by his voice that he was pleased she had turned to him, and when he arrived in the pick-up, sounding the horn outside the front door, he looked more like his old self.

'Lachie's Taxis,' he intoned. 'Good, reliable service.'

'The last time you said that, we broke down half a mile up the road.' Kate giggled.

'Yes, but I fixed it myself in no time.'

'Nearly an hour and a half.'

'Stop arguing,' he told her jokingly, and they drove towards Meadowpark.

The farm seemed to be much busier and more alive, Kate thought, as they drove along beside the barn and parked the pick-up. The concrete paths had been swept, and there was a warm, cosy smell of baking as they reached the kitchen door.

Kate banged on the door, and a few moments later it flew open and a young girl stared at them. She was slender and graceful, with brown curly hair and blue eyes. Kate vaguely remembered her as a child at Gemma's wedding.

'Yes?' she asked.

'I'm Kate, Gemma's sister,' she said. 'This is a friend of mine, Lachie Fraser. I suppose you must be Alec's cousin, Moira.'

'Yes, Moira Johnstone,' the girl said.

The ready colour rushed into her cheeks, as she looked back to see where Gemma was, then her blue eyes went to Lachie and it seemed as though she never wanted to look away.

# An Unexpected Caller

Kate smiled as Moira Johnstone stood aside to allow them to walk into the big farmhouse kitchen.

'Gemma has gone upstairs. I've just put Norman to bed and she's reading a story to him,' Moira said. 'I was just making a cup of tea. Gemma will be down in a minute. Perhaps you'd like a cup. Kate and Mr Fraser?'

Her eyes went again to Lachie's tall, rugged figure, though there was no answering smile in his eyes.

'Lachie,' he said quietly. 'You'd better call me Lachie, or you might confuse me with my brother, Angus.'

'Lachie,' Moira said, smiling shyly. 'Do you take sugar?'

'Two, please, though we can't stay for long, can we, Kate? I've got to get back. There's rather a lot to do.'

'Oh, of course.' Kate hurriedly rose

to her feet. Lachie hadn't mentioned that he was in a hurry. 'I'll just run upstairs and collect my things.'

She tiptoed quietly, so she didn't disturb Norrie, who used any excuse to leap out of bed after he had been tucked up for the night.

Picking up her cases, Kate slipped back downstairs, only to find Moira and Lachie regarding one another rather awkwardly.

'I'm sure your job must be fascinating, Mr Fraser — sorry, Lachie.' Moira was saying hesitantly. 'I suppose you'll have to protect and care for all the wild life in the woods. I've heard that poachers can do a lot of damage.'

'That's true,' Lachie agreed, though he volunteered no information. He wasn't usually so reticent, thought Kate, looking at his closed face. Yet Moira was obviously making a big effort to conquer her own shyness, and to make friends.

A moment later Gemma walked into the room, closing the door very quietly.

'That's Norrie off to sleep,' she said with obvious relief.

She was looking quite a lot better, Kate thought, eyeing her sister anxiously. Having Moira here was going to help enormously.

'Hello, you two.' Gemma smiled. 'Can you stay to supper?'

'Sorry,' Kate told her after a short pause. 'Lachie has to get back.'

She would have enjoyed a little while in the company of her sister and Moira Johnstone. It might have been nice to get to know the young girl better, but already Lachie was looking round.

'Shall I put your cases in the pick-up?' he asked Kate.

'If it's all part of Lachie's Taxi Service,' she teased, then rose to her feet with resignation when he made no reply.

'Oh well, I'll pop over another evening, Gemma. It's lovely to have you here, Moira,' she said, turning to the other girl. 'And if I can help you with anything at all, just give me a ring.'

'Thanks, Kate.' The younger girl smiled. 'It's been nice meeting you, and Lachie.'

'Cheerio,' he shouted, and a moment later he was driving the pick-up towards the main road.

'You should have said you were busy, Lachie,' Kate said rather crossly as they drove back to Hazelbank.

'Oh, I can fit in enough time for you.'

'Moira Johnstone seems to be a nice girl, and very pretty,' Kate continued, glancing at him sideways. The young girl had obviously been attracted to him.

Lachie scowled. 'She's OK. I suppose.'

'Didn't you notice?'

'I'm not very interested in girls at the moment,' Lachie said flatly.

'Oh.' Kate sounded unhappy. He had tended to make that very clear at Meadowpark recently. She glanced again at Lachie, hoping that she wasn't to blame for his attitude. She was spared saying anything further as the pick-up drew into the gates of Hazel-bank.

'I'll see you some time,' she said, getting out of the pick-up, while Lachie carried her cases to the door.

She would only make things worse, she decided, if she tried to talk to him about her fears.

'Thanks for your help, Lachie.'

'You know you've only got to ask,' he told her, and she sighed a little as she walked into the house after he had driven away. Lachie was so very different from Angus.

★  ★  ★

Caroline was settling down at Hazel-bank and bringing her own touches in home-making to the old house. In spite of all her cleaning in the past, with Molly Simpson to help, Kate had to admit the house had never looked better than it did now.

'It's a talent,' she said to Caroline as she arrived home from the post office one evening. 'You've got it, Caroline, but I don't think I have.'

'What sort of talent, dear?'

'Home-making. I've never managed to make Hazelbank look like this.'

Caroline looked pleased.

'You will when you marry, one day, and have your own home. Not that I'm trying to get rid of you! I love having your company, Kate, but I think you know what I mean. Your very own home is always that bit more special.'

'Yes,' Kate said reflectively. Sometimes she had dreams of the future, but she couldn't see ahead very clearly, and her thoughts on what could come were always rather confused.

'Now that Mrs Simpson is back, I thought we could maybe have a little family party so we can show everyone the slides we took in France.' Caroline's voice broke into her thoughts. 'We could ask the Fraser boys and perhaps young Moira Johnstone?'

'That sounds lovely,' Kate said. 'We used to have friends in quite often when

— when Mother was alive,' she ended.

She was finding that Caroline preferred them to talk naturally about their family life as it had been before.

'I'll phone Sally, shall I? Or would you prefer to do it, Caroline?' she asked.

Her stepmother turned away a little.

'No, you do it, dear,' she said carefully. 'I'm sure Sally would prefer you to ask her.'

Sally was out when Kate phoned, but a cheerful girl who introduced herself as Marion asked her to ring back an hour later.

'Is everything all right at home?' Sally asked when Kate eventually reached her.

'Of course. I'm only ringing to see if you've got a free weekend in the near future.' Kate told her. 'We're planning a family reunion, with Father and Caroline showing the slides they took on their honeymoon. We just thought how nice it would be if we were all together again, even if it's just for one evening.'

'Oh . . . Kate . . . '

She was almost sure she heard a sob in Sally's voice, and Kate's eyes were dark with concern.

'Are you OK, Sally?' she asked. 'I mean, you're happy enough in London, aren't you? You know you've only got to say . . . '

'I'm fine, absolutely OK,' Sally assured her and this time her voice was firm.

Had Kate imagined that husky note in her sister's voice?

'Then when would it be OK?' Kate asked. If she could get Sally home again, she would soon know whether her sister was happy or not.

'I won't manage home for ages,' Sally said airily. 'Sorry about that. Kate, but I'm very busy. You've no idea how much there is to do in London. I just won't be able to fit it in at the moment.'

'Oh, that's disappointing.' Her sister really did seem to have her time taken up. She waited for Sally to speak but there was silence.

'OK, Sally,' she said at length. 'Keep in touch, won't you?'

'Give . . . give them all my love,' Sally said quickly, and hung up.

Kate turned away from the phone and went into the sitting-room, where her father and Caroline were enjoying a cup of coffee. Caroline bent forward and poured out another cup.

'Keith has deserted us,' she said. 'He and Angus are working rather late this evening.'

'Everyone seems to be busy,' Kate said, 'even Sally, She's booked up for weeks ahead, and can't arrange a free weekend. I'm afraid we'll have to have our party without Sally.'

The smile left Caroline's eyes and she leaned forward again to fill up Gavin's cup.

'I would have thought she could arrange something,' Gavin Reid said with annoyance. 'She had no need to go rushing off like that. She might have waited until Caroline and I came home at least. I could have had a word with her . . . '

'More sugar, dear?' Caroline asked quietly, and Kate could see the shadows on her face. Was Caroline concerned in case her father upset himself, she wondered.

'Oh, Sally's fine, Dad,' she said quickly. 'No need to worry about her. We'll just have the party without her, won't we, Caroline?'

'Of course,' Caroline said. 'Why not?'

★　★　★

The following morning Keith was almost ready to leave for work, when Kate ran lightly downstairs.

'You're early, or have I slept in? What does the kitchen clock say?' she asked.

'That I'm early,' Keith smiled. 'Angus and I are hoping to have a quick run over to West Lodge. We've promised Mr Richmond that we'll start work on it this week.' His eyes grew serious. 'Angus might be a bit tired, though.

He's been working very hard on old Mrs Clark's cottage. He should be finished there this evening . . . '

He glanced round quickly as they heard the sound of a door opening upstairs. Kate and Caroline had been very firm with Gavin Reid, and had managed to make him promise to stay away from the office for the present. They were both determined he should be completely restored to health before going back to work.

Now Keith and Kate waited anxiously to hear if he was about to come down the stairs. If Gavin Reid suspected that Keith and Angus were having to work so hard, he might even now break his promise.

But a moment later the door shut again and the young people breathed a sigh of relief.

'I'll see you later then, Keith,' Kate said. 'Didn't you want that piece of toast?'

'It's gone leathery.'

'It will do for me. If I don't hurry up,

I'm going to be late! I've got much further to go than you.'

That evening, as Kate walked home, she saw a small crowd of people outside old Mrs Clark's cottage, among them Molly Simpson, who beckoned to her excitedly.

Angus stood in the centre of the crowd, warm rich colour in his cheeks, though there was a smile of mingled pleasure and embarrassment on his face.

'It's a marvellous job you've made of it, Mr Fraser,' Joe Thomson, Mrs Clark's other neighbour, was saying. 'We've watched you working here for Mrs Clark, and all in your own time, too.'

He looked round the assembled neighbours, clearing his throat. 'We won't forget it, I can tell you.'

'I'll never forget how good he's been to me,' old Mrs Clark said, wiping her eyes. 'My house would just have fallen down if it hadn't been for Angus . . .'

'Nonsense!' he protested. 'We'd have

done something about it.'

'No, it was in a bad state, as I can swear to,' put in Bob Simpson. 'Mr Fraser deserves all the thanks we can give him.'

Suddenly Angus spotted Kate on the fringe of the group, and the colour deepened on his face.

'Well . . . it's all finished now,' he said awkwardly. 'I need no more thanks than to see you all standing round here, more out of neighbourliness towards Mrs Clark I'm sure, than to pay me compliments. I'm just glad I was able to help. Now, if you'll excuse me . . . '

Joe Thomson and his wife were looking round at their neighbours with smiles, as he put a small parcel into old Mrs Clark's hands.

'Er . . . if you can just spare us another minute,' he explained. 'We're all very happy about how you've helped our neighbour, Mr Fraser, so we passed round the hat. Give him the parcel, Mrs Clark. He fully deserves it.'

The old woman smiled proudly as

she handed Angus a slender gift-wrapped box.

'Oh.' Angus looked taken aback. 'Really — what's this?'

He opened the box, taking out a lovely fountain pen. Angus was almost too moved to speak for a moment.

'Do you like it, Angus?' old Mrs Clark asked, and he bent down and kissed her cheek.

Looking on, Kate felt a rush of warmth in her own heart.

'It's terrific,' he said. 'I'll always treasure it.'

\* \* \*

A moment later Angus slipped through the small group.

'I . . . I feel I don't deserve this,' he said to Kate. 'They're all giving me more credit than is due.'

'I don't think so,' Kate assured him. 'I'm so glad old Mrs Clark's cottage is sorted out now, though. How did you get on at West Lodge, Angus? Keith mentioned you were going there today.'

The smile left his eyes.

'Ah, now that's a different story entirely,' he said, falling into step beside her. 'We've got some problems there. Not that they can't be overcome!' he assured her stoutly, when he saw the concern on her face.

'It's just some panelling that needs to be restored. Tom Andrews could have done it, but Tom's abroad now. We miss him a lot. He was the only one, besides your father, who was really skilled in tackling that sort of thing.'

'And now you're realising that the only one who can do the panelling at West Lodge is my father. Is that it, Angus?'

'Something like that.' He nodded soberly. 'But I'm well aware of the state of his health, Kate. Keith and I had a long discussion about it this afternoon. Bob Simpson's had a look at the panelling, and he chickened out almost at once, though I think Bob could do part of it at least. Well . . . maybe a little bit.'

'What about you?' asked Kate. 'Couldn't you do it?'

For a while he walked on in silence.

'I could tackle part of it,' he admitted honestly. 'At a pinch, I would have a go at all of it, though . . . though I haven't got anything like the skill of Tom Andrews, or your father. My own particular skills don't really lie in carving.'

He broke off abruptly, and Kate squeezed his arm as she remembered the art course he had taken in London, then had to give up.

Now and again she could see how much it must have meant to Angus to have failed in his art.

'Don't breathe a word to your father just yet,' he told her.

'Of course I won't. That's for you and Keith to do when you decide it's necessary.'

They stood for a moment where the path divided towards Hazelbank and the gamekeeper's cottage.

'I shouldn't have told you. It will only worry you,' Angus said contritely.

'No, I'm so glad you did,' Kate told him. 'I'm pleased that you should confide in me.'

Angus looked at her rather strangely for a moment, then he turned away after wishing her good night. Kate walked on home, deep in thought.

★  ★  ★

There was a car outside the front door at Hazelbank and Kate found Caroline preparing a tray of coffee and sandwiches.

'An old friend of your father has come to see him,' she said. 'I think it's a gentlemen's party rather than mixed, so I'm taking this tray into the study.'

'Is Keith in there as well?' Kate asked.

'No, he phoned to say he'll be working for another hour yet. He has some paperwork to do.'

'He works too hard,' Kate said. 'Everyone seems to be working like slaves trying to put the company back on an even keel.'

'Ssh!' whispered Caroline. 'Don't even mention it in case your father ever decides to sneak up on us at the time. I'm terrified he'll overhear something!'

'Sorry,' Kate said. 'I won't put my foot in it, I promise you.'

It was another hour before the study door opened and Gavin Reid emerged with a tall, white-haired man.

Kate could hear his hearty voice talking reassuringly to her father as they walked towards the front door.

'It's Mr Sproat,' she said, 'from the timber merchants. Dad has been dealing with them for years. He gets very special wood from them, as I remember. I met Mr Sproat once or twice when he called at our workshop.'

Her eyes met Caroline's anxiously, then a moment later the door opened and Gavin Reid stood there, his face very stern and white.

'Is Keith home yet?' he asked.

'Not yet, Dad,' Kate said quickly. 'He . . . he's working late.'

'Are you all right, darling?' Caroline Reid was asking anxiously.

'I think I'll feel better after I've had a word with Keith,' Gavin Reid said. 'I'll just phone him, and ask him to bring the books home with him. There are one or two matters that could do with straightening out.'

Caroline and Kate looked at one another with dismay as they heard Gavin Reid phoning Keith.

A moment later they heard the sound of the study door closing quietly.

'I think Mr Sproat must have said something to Dad,' Kate said, her eyes wide and anxious. 'I got a horrible feeling that he's just learned that all is not well.'

Caroline Reid frowned.

'He has to know some time,' she said quietly. 'We can just hope that he's well enough to learn all the facts.'

A short time later Keith slipped into

the kitchen by the back door, his briefcase bulging, and extra files under his arm.

'Did you tell him?' he asked Kate anxiously.

'No, I suspect it was Mr Sproat from the timber merchant's.'

Keith slapped a hand to his forehead.

'I meant to get a cheque away to them this week, but I didn't get round to it. He's one of the few still waiting for their accounts to be cleared. I'm gradually working my way through them, but it's slow work until we get paid for work we've done.'

He rumpled a hand through his hair, his young face white.

'I . . . I don't know how to start telling him,' he said.

Caroline Reid put her arms round him and gave him a warm and comforting hug.

'Gavin is used to assessing the situation from his own books, darling,' she said gently. 'Just give him the books, and leave it to him.'

'But . . . '

'So there you are! And you've brought the books, Keith, fine. I'll just take them into the study, if you don't mind.'

All three whirled round as Gavin Reid appeared at the kitchen door.

'Bernard Sproat is a very old friend,' he said quietly. 'I was surprised when I learned that his account hasn't been paid for some months, Keith. But no doubt there is some sort of explanation.'

Keith's face was now very white as he handed over the books. Once more Gavin Reid disappeared into his study while his family stared at one another.

In an odd sort of way, it was a relief, yet they were apprehensive about the effects such a shock could have on him.

'I should have told him myself, quietly,' Caroline said. 'I never thought of anyone calling on him like this. I thought it would be safe to keep him in the dark, as long as he didn't go near the workshop.'

'We all tried to shield him, Caroline,' Kate tried to reassure her, 'and Keith most of all. I think he has been marvellous to carry on the way he has done.'

'Thanks, Kate,' Keith said tiredly. 'It doesn't change things, though, and I know how many mistakes I've made. I . . . I think I'll go for a walk.'

'Not before you have something to eat!' his mother cried.

'I don't want anything!' And the door banged behind him.

★   ★   ★

Gavin Reid heard the faint bang of the door as he began to study his firm's books, starting from the time his severe illness had forced him to give up his work temporarily.

He was well used to reading the pattern of his business, and gradually the whole picture began to unfold before him. His illness had brought a lack of clarity in thought, and it was mainly his own actions which had brought on most of the ills of the company.

He had expected a mere boy, like Keith, to take up where he left off, and run the company even though he had no experience. His own experience had only been gained over many years.

He shook his head a little over some of the decisions Keith had made, then smiled when he saw that his mistakes had been realised and brave attempts had been made to put them right.

Keith might have succeeded, too, if everything had gone on without mishap. But the books showed the disastrous effects of rising prices, increased wages, and the gaps made when some of his best men left the firm. He could, perhaps, have had some influence there, if he hadn't been lying on his hospital bed.

Gavin Reid shook his head again, as he followed the pattern of his declining business, biting his lip when he realised how worried his young stepson must have been, and how valiantly he had managed to hide the truth.

Angus Fraser's return had been a godsend, and must have been a great relief to Keith.

The two young men had obviously taken hold of the company, and jobs were now being completed much more quickly, and costed to make a profit instead of, in many cases, a loss.

It hadn't been Keith's fault, thought Gavin, laying aside the last of the books. It had been his own fault for expecting too much of his stepson, but the fact remained that the firm's financial position was not at its best.

Caroline Reid, in a soft blue house-coat, tapped lightly on the door and came in carrying a small tray of hot malted milk and a plate of biscuits. She had a look of determination combined with anxiety in her eyes.

'Don't you think you'd better come upstairs to bed, Gavin?' she asked. 'Haven't you done enough?'

'I guess so, but I'll want to have a

word with you all in the morning.'

'It can all keep until then,' Caroline said soothingly.

She didn't mention that Keith had come home, worn out, and that Kate still sat, wrapped in her warm dressing-gown, beside the dying embers of the kitchen fire.

Gavin Reid rose to his feet, his body stiff with weariness. He hadn't realised that he had worked so late until he heard the hall clock chiming two.

Even as Caroline put out a hand towards him, he stumbled a little and with a small cry, she guided him towards a chair.

# His Sacrifice

Caroline Reid looked round anxiously as she heard Kate coming swiftly into the room. The girl's face went white when she saw her father leaning back in his chair, Caroline bending over him.

'It's all right,' her stepmother said quickly, her practised fingers on Gavin Reid's pulse. 'He's just a little bit weak from over-tiring himself. Get Keith, please. I think the quicker we get him up to bed, the better.'

Keith had been apprehensive about facing his stepfather again, but now all business worries were forgotten as he hurried downstairs.

The following morning it was Keith who was first to come downstairs. He had spent a troubled night, and he knew he would have no peace of mind until he and Gavin had gone into the whole question of their business difficulties.

Long before eight o'clock, however, the rest of the family appeared in the kitchen, with Gavin Reid looking much better for his night's rest.

'Your father is a very stubborn man,' Caroline Reid said, smiling ruefully at Kate. 'I wanted him to stay in bed this morning . . . '

'But he's fed up playing the invalid,' Gavin Reid finished. 'I promise to go to bed early at night, but there are things I want sorted out first.'

As Caroline Reid poured tea and they all helped themselves to breakfast, her husband showed just how well he knew his own firm by giving a quick resumé as to how it stood.

'Not good,' he ended, 'but a great deal better than it was.'

'I know,' Keith said miserably. 'But only thanks to Angus . . . '

'Let's get one thing straight, Keith,' his stepfather said firmly. 'I know my business inside out, and you can stop blaming yourself. I should never have expected it of you.'

Keith flushed. 'I made such stupid mistakes,' he mumbled. 'When I look back on it . . . ' His voice tailed off.

'You would have made different decisions?' asked his stepfather.

'Of course I would.'

'That's because you're now a great deal more experienced. I think you did wonders struggling on with it at all. I can only thank you from the bottom of my heart that I have got a business to save.'

Keith brightened. 'I'm sure we'll manage to put things straight,' he said more eagerly. 'The contract for West Lodge is a very good one, and I'm sure others might arise from it. We'll just have to work twice as hard to pull it all together, and I'm sure we'll make it with Angus's help.'

'I'm sure we will,' Gavin Reid agreed.

'I can manage with less, Gavin,' Mrs Reid said readily.

'And perhaps I could contribute

more,' Kate offered, but her father smiled and shook his head.

'You both do more than enough already. We will have to cut our standard of living a little, but not drastically just yet. I've really made the position clear to you all so that, as a family, we can shoulder it together. We can't have Keith worrying about this on his own.'

Keith's small sigh of relief was heartfelt, and he had a new spring in his step as he went to collect his briefcase. It would be a relief to Angus, too, to know that Gavin Reid was aware exactly how the business stood, and was taking it so well.

Kate, too, excused herself from the breakfast table.

'See you both this evening,' she said cheerfully.

Caroline Reid watched them go, then turned to look at her husband, whose face was once again white and tired.

'And now will you please have an extra hour or two in bed?' she asked, and he sighed deeply and nodded.

'I've married a very managing woman.'

'And I haven't even started yet,' she told him darkly.

★   ★   ★

In the evening, Caroline met Kate with a bright smile as soon as the girl walked into the kitchen. She was surrounded by books and lists.

'I'm working out lists here, and suggested menus,' she told Kate. 'I'll need some help.'

'What with?' Kate asked.

'The family party, of course. I think it's a good idea to go ahead with that. It should cheer us all up, and half the fun will be in having us all together again. It needn't cost a great deal.'

'Oh, lovely!' Kate exclaimed.

In spite of her father's cheerful mood that morning, Kate had had rather a depressing day. But now the warmth of the kitchen, with Caroline looking so happy, cheered her up considerably.

155

'Now, there's Gemma, Alec and young Norman. And we'll ask them to bring Moira with them. That's four so far.'

Kate helped herself to some delicious casserole, and sat down, offering one or two suggestions.

'Angus and Lachie as well,' she added.

'Angus and Lachie,' Caroline Reid agreed, then paused. 'But not Sally?'

'I doubt it,' Kate said. 'You know, I'm worried about Sally. I'm not sure she's happy in London, though I don't know why she stays there if she doesn't like it.'

'Don't you?' Caroline asked carefully. Kate looked up at her stepmother quickly, but the serious expression had gone.

'Should we sit down to supper, or have a buffet?' she asked, the subject changed.

'Dad likes to sit down, because he says he can't manage a wee plate,' Kate told her.

Caroline laughed. 'That settles it, then.'

For a long time Caroline Reid stared out of the kitchen window after Kate had gone upstairs. It would be nice to have Angus, Lachie and Moira Johnstone, but the family would still be incomplete if Sally couldn't be with them.

Kate hadn't seen Angus for several days, though she knew he was spending most of his time at West Lodge.

Keith and Gavin Reid now discussed the business more openly in the evenings, and she couldn't help being aware of the problems of restoration work.

Kate was kept busy with her job in the post office, however, and she wore her usual cheerful smile for her customers as she stamped pension books and weighed parcels.

'Excuse me, miss, I wonder if you can help me. Do you happen to know where I can find Mr Angus Fraser?'

Kate's heart leapt a little, and she

looked up quickly. She hadn't noticed the tall, white-haired stranger until he stood in front of her.

'Angus?' she asked. 'Of course I can help you.'

Quickly she gave him directions, then drew forward a pad and pencil, drawing a small map as she gave the stranger directions once again.

'If you follow that, you can't go wrong, though I doubt if he'll be at home until this evening. He just might be in the workshop — that's it over there.' Kate pointed to a spot on the map she had drawn.

'You seem to know him pretty well.' The man smiled.

'Well, we've been friends since childhood. Are you one of his friends from London?'

'No, I haven't met Mr Fraser,' the elderly man said. 'I'm interested in his art, especially his wildlife studies. I expect you'll be even more familiar with his work than I am.'

Kate smiled. It always gave her

pleasure to hear of someone who appreciated Angus's talent.

'His wildlife pictures are marvellous,' she agreed. 'I honestly don't know what people in London expect. He didn't make it down there. I'm sure he's much better than some people who do succeed, yet Angus had to come home because he failed.'

The tall man stared at her.

'I'm afraid we're at cross purposes now. I represent a large chemical corporation and we're very interested in conservation.

'We are planning an exhibition in London which will feature a new plant we are opening in Brazil, and we would like to commission Angus Fraser to paint a series of wildlife pictures for the exhibition.

'Surely he's working on that sort of thing — professionally, I mean?'

Kate stared at the man uncomprehendingly. They were at cross purposes. He expected Angus to be working professionally on his art!

The post office bell clanged, and another spate of customers appeared.

'I'm sorry, Mr . . . '

'Bailey. Desmond Bailey.'

'I'm sorry, Mr Bailey,' Kate repeated. 'But you'll have to talk to Angus about it.'

'Of course. Is there a hotel where I can check in? I'll have to stay overnight at least.'

Kate gave him further directions, then turned to her customers, trying to bring her mind back to the job.

According to Mr Bailey, Angus hadn't failed in London. In fact, he had succeeded so well that this man had travelled from the South to offer him a commission.

Judging by his questions, he had come expecting Angus to take on the work, yet Angus had gone back to work, doing something quite different.

Why had he done that? Had Angus known that the company was in trouble? Did the family mean so much to Angus that he had given up an extremely promising career in order to help out?

Kate felt a lump in her throat as she thought of his sacrifice. Somehow she knew she had to thank him, tell him how much his efforts had been appreciated.

★　★　★

Gavin Reid listened to Kate in amazement when she told him of the day's events.

'You mean Angus gave up everything to come back here?' he asked.

Kate nodded.

'But why? And you say this Mr Bailey wants to offer Angus a commission for a series of pictures,' he mused, 'for an industrial company.'

'Yes,' Kate said, 'though I'm not very clear what it all involves. Something about Angus having to go to Brazil to paint the wildlife. I felt sort of stunned when he talked about Angus's work, and seemed to expect that he was

161

painting professionally.

'I . . . I can't understand it. Why should Angus pretend to fail when he was really on his way to a brilliant career? From what Mr Bailey said, he'd got his diploma in fine art, too. It doesn't make sense.'

'Hmm.' Gavin Reid stared at his daughter.

'Mr Bailey will be seeing Angus tonight,' he murmured. 'Very well. I'll ring him in the morning, and see what has come of it all. No point in speculating until then.'

'No, I suppose not,' Kate said, though something about the whole situation made her feel uneasy. There was something here she just didn't understand.

'Are the menfolk quite adventurous over their food?' Caroline Reid asked, coming into the room and interrupting her thoughts.

'I mean, do they like to try one or two exotic dishes, perhaps, or has it to be good, plain stuff?'

Mrs Reid's smile wavered when she saw Kate so preoccupied.

'Oh.' Kate turned to her with a smile. 'Sorry, I was thinking. No, they prefer fairly simple things, but you can use all your imagination on the sweet. Oh, and we'd better have something simple for Norrie. Jelly and custard will suit him very well, or I'll make him a pear boat.'

'You . . . er . . . aren't worried about anything, are you?' Caroline asked. She had been out when Kate and her father talked.

'Just something to do with Angus,' Kate told her, 'I expect it will all be sorted out tomorrow.'

Caroline Reid nodded, though her eyes rested thoughtfully on her stepdaughter. Kate was a lovely girl and no doubt she would fall in love one day, though she never gave any hint as to how she felt about anyone, or indeed, if there was anyone.

*   *   *

Gavin Reid asked Angus to come and see him at ten o'clock the following morning — without fail.

'I really ought to be up at West Lodge.' Angus had protested on the telephone.

'West Lodge can keep for an hour,' came the reply. 'There's something I want to talk to you about, Angus.'

Angus had heard that note in Mr Reid's voice before, and it brooked no argument.

'Very well,' he said quietly.

Gavin Reid had told his wife a little about it, and she prepared a tray with coffee and biscuits, then left the men to talk things over in the lounge. She, too, had often wondered why Angus had come back to work here.

Had Angus perhaps returned home for the sake of her stepdaughter?

Gavin Reid lost no time in coming to the point. Angus looked very taken aback, though he quickly recovered.

'You allowed me to think you had failed,' the older man said quietly. 'But now we have someone coming north to see you, and offer you a commission.'

'How did you find out?' Angus asked.

'Mr Bailey called in at the post office, and asked Kate where to find you.'

'I see. He said nothing about that to me. But you can forget about it, Mr Reid. I've told Mr Bailey I can't accept the commission.'

'Can't accept!' Gavin Reid cried angrily. 'Why not, Angus?'

The young man's cheeks coloured. He had worked very hard at trying to perfect his technique in carving out the panelling for West Lodge. Bob Simpson had also had a go, but Bob had been quite right in knowing his own limitations. He hadn't the necessary skill to do the work required. Angus knew there was no-one to do it except himself.

'I . . . I'm out of practice. I . . . well . . . I'd just be no good at it. Mr Reid, and think how terrible it would be if I made a mess of it.

'I mean, there's a deadline to the

commission, and if I failed, they would find it difficult to get someone else to do the pictures in time. It just wouldn't be fair.'

'That's nonsense, and you know it,' Gavin said. 'I think you'd better try again. Angus. I didn't help you through college — well, we won't say anything about that — '

Gavin Reid bit back the words. It seemed a long time ago now since he had found out that Angus had a chance to study in London and was refusing the opportunity because of the cost involved.

But Gavin had thought Angus would be unfair to himself if he didn't take the opportunity when it was available. He had managed, after a lengthy argument, to persuade Angus to accept his financial support.

'I'll pay you back one day,' Angus had vowed.

'You'll repay me tenfold if you make a success of your career,' Gavin Reid told him.

To himself he had sworn never to mention the matter, but now it had slipped out, and Angus leapt to his feet.

'Oh yes, we will,' he said. 'You did help me, Mr Reid, and you'll never know what you did for me. Even if I never paint another picture. I know deep inside me that I can do it now.

'I've had my training, and it's something no-one can ever take away from me. But when I heard about your business . . . '

'Who told you?' Gavin asked sharply.

Angus bit his lip. His cheeks were now scarlet with embarrassment.

'I . . . I saw Keith in London,' he said painfully. 'He came down just before your wedding, and he was worried then.'

'I know all about it, as you well know by now. I made him bring home the books, and I was going to discuss it with both of you as soon as I felt able to take an active part in the business again. I rather think that's going to be fairly soon now . . . '

'Oh, no, Mr Reid, you aren't fit yet.' Angus protested. 'Not yet, anyway. I've been trying out a bit of that panelling, and I know just how much is involved. You're going to need me to do that panelling.'

Gavin Reid looked into the young man's earnest hazel eyes while he drummed his fingers on the chair, a sure sign he was thinking deeply.

'What does this commission involve, Angus?' he asked.

Angus was silent for a moment, then his eyes began to shine with eagerness.

'It's a series of ten pictures depicting Brazilian wildlife in all its forms. There are also photographic studies as well. I would have to go to Brazil for about three months in order to do the work.

'The chemical company are a huge concern and employ a lot of people, and like many others these days are keen on conservation. They put on exhibitions to show how their chemicals can be employed to help save wildlife. It saves people from getting the wrong

168

ideas about them.

'They would show large photographs of their new plant, and exhibit my contributions, which would later hang in their main offices.'

'What would you paint?' Gavin asked with absorbed interest.

'Oh, I'd do birds, butterflies, fish, plants and perhaps the lesser-known animals.'

'How long have you got before you decide?'

'I would have to fly to Brazil in about two months' time. It's far too little time, Mr Reid.'

'Nonsense,' Gavin said again, thumping his hand on the chair. 'Now listen to me. Angus, I'll never forget what a sacrifice you've made in trying to put the place in order, and succeeding.'

'We're not out of the wood yet . . . '

'But the business can be saved, thanks to you. I never considered you owed me anything for trying to help you. It's up to all of us to encourage talent wherever we find it, and I felt a privilege to have a hand helping you, Angus.

'Now the best way you can repay me is to accept this contract. Will you do that?'

Angus looked at the older man unhappily. He, not Gavin Reid, knew just how much work there was still to be done, but he was going to find it very difficult to explain. Somehow he was going to have to complete that panelling before taking up the Brazilian commission.

'Very well, Mr Reid,' he agreed. 'I'll phone Mr Bailey and tell him that I accept.'

'Good lad!' Gavin cried. 'And now let me shake you by the hand and congratulate you on your success. I'm very proud of you.'

Again Angus's eyes glowed, and in spite of his worries over the company there was a deep feeling of personal satisfaction. It would be wonderful to be able to paint those pictures. He knew he could put his heart into the work.

For a long moment after Angus had gone, Gavin Reid gazed out of the window towards his workshop. Somehow, he thought to himself, he must get back to work very soon.

★   ★   ★

Kate felt very subdued when she heard all about the sacrifice Angus had made for the firm.

She felt deeply indebted to him, though Angus seemed to avoid her as though he didn't want to discuss it.

She walked up to the farm to visit Gemma, then walked home again, relieved and happy that things seemed to be so much better for her sister at Meadowpark.

'Moira is knitting for me.' Gemma laughed. 'After she saw the mess I was producing with two needles and a ball of wool, she insisted on taking over.'

The young girl laughed shyly, and produced a tiny snowy-white garment.

'You knit beautifully,' Kate told her,

and Moira Johnstone coloured with pleasure.

'I'm doing a Fair Isle sweater for Norrie,' she said. 'I hope I can finish it in time for the party on Saturday.'

'I hope he can keep it clean.' Kate laughed, then turned to her sister more seriously. 'Can I phone Sally from here?' she asked. 'I wish she would make an effort to come home for the party. I think it would please Caroline so much.'

'Help yourself,' Gemma said, pointing to the telephone.

Kate dialled the number, letting it ring for a while, then put down the receiver.

'They must all be out,' she said briefly. 'Well, see you on Saturday. I'd better be on my way before it gets too late.'

The following evening Kate was busy in the kitchen when the back door opened, and Lachie's grinning face appeared, a brace of pheasants in his hand.

'I come bearing gifts,' he said, putting the pheasants down on the small table. 'My father asked Angus to bring these the other night, but he must have forgotten. They've been hung, by the way.'

'Oh, marvellous,' Kate said. 'I love pheasant. I'd better volunteer to do the plucking, though. Caroline is busy making sweets for Saturday.'

'Oh yes, I'm looking forward to that. Kate, what do you think of this new commission Angus has been offered? He may have to go to Brazil.'

Kate had turned away, not wishing Lachie to see the sudden bleak look in her eyes. Somehow Brazil seemed very far away.

'I know. Excuse me a minute, Lachie . . . '

The phone was ringing loudly, and Kate hurried to answer it. It was a moment before she recognised Moira's clear young voice.

'Hello, Kate?'

'Yes.'

'I . . . I don't want to worry you, but is Norman with you?' Moira asked.

Kate's heart lurched.

'Norrie? No, Moira, he isn't here. Why?'

'He was playing outside and I just went into the kitchen to prepare his supper, when he just vanished.

'Alec and Gemma have gone to visit friends. Oh, Kate. I . . . I don't know what to do. I seem to have been looking for him for ages . . . '

# Little Boy Lost

Kate's mouth felt dry as she heard the rising hysteria in Moira's voice. Obviously the young girl was near to panic at the thought that Norman was lost.

'Stay there!' Kate said urgently. 'Don't wander about looking for him any more. I'll be right over.'

'Oh, thanks, Kate,' Moira said with heartfelt relief.

Kate hurried back to the sitting-room, where Lachie was flicking through a magazine.

'That was Moira,' she said breathlessly. 'She's been looking after Norrie while Gemma and Alec are out and he's gone missing. Lachie. Could you take me up there in the pick-up straight-away?'

Lachie wasted no time in asking questions, though his eyes showed his alarm. Kate put a hand on his arm as they heard Caroline Reid coming back into the kitchen.

'Not a word,' she said to Lachie. 'I don't want Dad or Caroline worried needlessly. We'll try to find Norrie ourselves first.'

Caroline Reid came out into the hall as Kate hurriedly donned her coat, her lips slightly stiff as she forced a smile.

'Oh, Caroline, we — we're just going out. We won't be long.'

'That's all right, dear.'

She stood at the door, watching them leave, then she wandered back into the kitchen.

Kate had been tense, and once again Caroline Reid felt shut out. Perhaps Kate and Lachie were just going out on a date, she thought. Then her brows wrinkled again.

No, there had been an urgency in both of them, yet Kate had said nothing to her. There were times when Caroline Reid felt on the outside of things.

The doorbell shrilled, and Mrs Reid wiped her hands on a kitchen towel and pulled off her apron.

Opening the door, she gasped with surprise when she saw Sally standing on the doorstep, and for a long moment they stared at one another.

'Hello,' said Sally, forcing a bright smile. 'Aren't you going to let me come in?'

The words were like a cool breath on Caroline Reid's face and nervously she stood aside.

For a brief moment her heart had pounded with hope, as she wondered if Sally had changed her mind about coming to the family reunion.

Then she saw the faintly aggressive look in the girl's eyes, and realised that Sally was here for her own reasons, not because she wanted to please her stepmother.

She didn't see the slight trembling of Sally's mouth as she walked into the old familiar home, which now looked strangely unfamiliar.

Sally had expected Kate to be there, ready and willing to hug her, and perhaps chide her a little in the way which the younger girl had always found reassuring.

But, instead, it was her new step-mother who looked at her with reserve and lack of warmth.

Sally felt as though her basic security had been shaken.

'I . . . I'm just making things for the party,' Caroline Reid said, leading the way into the kitchen. 'Your father has gone out to see a friend, and he should be home in a moment. Kate . . . er, Kate is out with Lachie.'

'With Lachie?' Sally asked. She would have expected her to be out with Angus.

The older woman nodded nervously. She was far from being at her ease with her youngest stepdaughter.

'Would you like something to eat now?' she asked.

'I ate on the train. Just you carry on, I can always get myself something later, if I may,' she added, remembering that the kitchen was now her stepmother's domain.

'Of course,' Caroline Reid assured her politely. If Keith had come home like this, she would have wanted to sit him down and cosset him a little, but Sally might resent that sort of attention.

On the other hand, the girl looked tired and depressed. She was about to insist on her having something when the door opened and Gavin Reid walked in.

'Sally!' he cried.

'Hello, Dad,' she said, looking up at him rather carefully, then her face crumpled and he came to take her in his arms.

Again Caroline Reid watched, seeing that Sally's brightness was all on the exterior. Underneath she was just a very young girl, but it took her father to bring this out.

'Why on earth did you rush away to London the way you did?' he was asking. 'Just when my back was turned.

I felt very annoyed with you, Sally. We both did — didn't we, Caroline?'

'We — we must allow Sally to be independent, dear,' she said levelly.

'She's got plenty of time before she becomes independent. Well? Have you had your tea?'

'Well, no, not yet,' his wife replied, and Gavin groaned a little.

'I think she needs something to warm her up,' he said briefly.

'You look cold and peaky, darling. I think I'd better hear all about what you're doing in London.'

Caroline Reid was quietly setting the kitchen table. She had prided herself that she would never fail Gavin as a wife. But suppose she failed him as a stepmother?

*  *  *

Kate was unaware of anything other than her own deep anxiety as she and Lachie arrived at Meadowpark. Moira opened the door to them, her small

180

white face tear stained, her short hair disarrayed.

'Oh, thank goodness you're here,' she cried, her eyes going to Lachie. 'Both of you! I — I'm so frightened. I've looked everywhere, and banged the old cowbell. It's a sort of game, Norrie always comes if you do that. It means he can have milk and biscuits . . . '

'Well, take it easy, Moira,' Lachie said calmly, and the girl seemed to relax a little.

'We'll search, too,' Kate comforted her. 'Sometimes you miss something when you're close to it. Lachie and I may notice something new.

'We'll start on the house, Lachie, and then we'll try the outbuildings. He might have crept under a bed or something, playing hide and seek with himself, and fallen asleep. I've known that to happen before now.'

Together they searched every room, looking in every cupboard — but Kate had an empty feeling inside, as though she knew the child was not in the house.

'We'd better start on the barn and the old stables now,' she said to Lachie. 'We — we'd better look at the old water wheel . . .'

They looked briefly at one another, then looked away. The water wheel had not been used for years, and Alec kept the access doors well bolted from his small adventurous son, but each of them was well aware of the danger in exploring the huge wheel.

A moment later, however, a car swung into the yard and Gemma and Alec climbed out, their faces bright with happiness. They were talking excitedly, but their voices tailed off as they saw Moira, Kate and Lachie standing by the door.

'What's happened?' Gemma asked, running forward as she sensed their apprehension.

Moira burst into tears again, and it was Kate who took Gemma's hand, telling her as gently as she could, afraid of what the shock might do.

'We haven't looked around yet,' Lachie said easily. 'He's probably not far away.'

Gemma turned to Moira, her eyes suddenly darkened with fear.

'You were supposed to be looking after him,' she cried. 'If I had known . . . '

'Don't blame Moira,' Lachie said, stepping forward. 'Norrie's a real boy, and we all know that boys get up to mischief, especially round a farm. Angus and I were always in hot water at his age. Norrie could give anybody the slip these days.'

'Of course he can,' Alec said, coming to put his arms round Gemma. 'Don't worry, darling. Lachie and I will find him.'

Moira stared after Lachie gratefully as both men went off in the direction of the barn.

'I — I'm so sorry, Gemma,' she whispered.

'Oh, it isn't your fault,' Gemma

whispered dully. 'It's just that I'm frightened.' She turned to Kate.

'I know, but we'll give the men a chance to look for him.'

Lachie and Alec searched every inch around the old water wheel.

'He — he can't have fallen down underneath, can he?' asked Alec fearfully, speaking more to himself than Lachie. 'Every access point was locked and barred. We would need lights, Lachie.'

Lachie nodded, and together the two men went back into the yard.

A small kitten ran out of the barn and Lachie paused, remembering Norrie's love for them. Perhaps Norrie was with them.

'Wait a minute, Alec,' he said. 'We never really moved everything in the barn.'

Together both men hurried back into the barn, where they lifted bales of hay aside.

Suddenly Lachie saw Norrie's red sandal sticking out from a warm nest of hay. The child was sound asleep, curled up beside a family of small kittens, who were immediately protected by their mother as Alec thankfully picked up the sleeping child and Lachie replaced the bales of hay.

Norrie cried a little as his father carried him over to the farmhouse, calling reassuringly to Gemma. But it was Moira who ran forward and took the sleeping child, her face shining with gratitude, while Alec looked after Gemma, making her a hot, sweet drink.

There were no words to express how they all felt, but their looks said it all.

'Will you two stay for a quick supper?' Alec asked, turning to Kate and Lachie.

'No, we'd best get back,' Kate said after looking questioningly at Lachie. 'I expect Dad and Caroline will wonder where I am!'

Kate said good night to Lachie as he drew up outside the front door.

'Sure you won't come in for a nightcap?' she asked.

'Quite sure,' he said. 'Do you realise what time a gamekeeper has to rise in the morning?'

'Oh, you poor thing,' said Kate banteringly, then squeezed his fingers. 'Thanks, Lachie.'

★ ★ ★

Kate heard Sally's voice the moment she opened the door and almost ran into the sitting-room, where the family had gathered round the fire.

'Sally! You made it after all! I've been trying to reach you on the phone, but I never thought of you being on your way.'

Sally had risen to greet her sister, her fingers clinging to Kate. The older girl, knowing her so well, was aware of the deep undercurrents in Sally and held her at arm's length, looking at her closely. But a signal seemed to pass between them, and Kate knew that she would have to speak to Sally later.

Keith, too, arrived home shortly

afterwards, and for a while Caroline Reid relaxed as conversation grew general, and the young people all laughed and talked happily together.

Gavin looked relaxed, leaning back in his chair with an air of contentment. This is how a family should be, thought his wife, then she saw that Sally's fingers were tightly clenched, and that Kate was eyeing her sister warily.

'I think we'll leave you young people to lock up,' she said, rising.

'Not even one late night?' asked Gavin Reid, grinning ruefully as he, too, stood up.

'Yes, but you must take things easy before the party, darling. Two late nights in a row isn't a good idea.'

'See how she bullies me?' Gavin Reid joked, grinning at Sally.

For a moment there was nothing but amusement in the young girl's eyes as they rested on her stepmother, then her smile faded and she looked away.

Quietly Caroline Reid took her husband's arm as they walked upstairs.

'I'll do the locking up,' Keith said a few minutes later, and the two girls were left alone.

'Well?' asked Kate.

'Well what?'

'Don't try telling me that everything in the garden is lovely. I know you too well, Sally, and you're never happy until you share things with someone.'

'I don't know what you're talking about,' Sally evaded, looking around for her handbag. 'I'm going up to bed. Caroline put the electric blanket on . . .'

'It will keep another minute. Come on, Sally. Can't I help?'

Kate waited for the usual tears which accompanied Sally's worries and disappointments, but this time Sally merely put on the bright smile she had worn for her stepmother.

'I'm fine,' she said airily. 'Home for the party, as you say. You practically order me to come home, then wonder what's wrong when I do! You know. Kate, a spell in London wouldn't do you any harm either.'

Keith had appeared in the doorway and Sally stared at him too.

'Or Keith,' she added. 'You're so naïve, both of you!'

She walked out of the room and Keith's eyes met Kate's, seeing the distress in them.

'She's just tired,' he said comfortingly. Yet he, too, could sense the change in the younger girl. Sally had grown older.

★   ★   ★

The following evening Hazelbank seemed to come to life as Caroline put the finishing touches to the table for the buffet supper, setting out a few beautiful flower arrangements.

The house shone with polish, the new curtains and cushions providing the touches of colour it needed to enhance the lovely old furniture, so that even Sally had to admit to herself that Hazelbank looked its best.

She had brought a very fashionable dress home with her to wear.

Caroline Reid wore one of her honeymoon dresses and Kate's choice of creamy white was perfect for her dark hair and eyes. Kate would look good in anything, thought Caroline Reid fondly. It was strange how three sisters could all be so different.

Gemma and Moira showed no signs of their anxious hours as they arrived with Alec carrying an excited Norrie. It had been arranged for him to stay the night in the cot which Kate kept for him in her bedroom.

Gemma was looking very well, having chosen a loose-fitting dress in dark russet brown instead of her usual pink, and Moira had set and combed out her fair hair.

Moira smiled shyly as she said hello to Sally.

'You live in London now, don't you?' she asked. 'Do you enjoy that?'

'It's great,' Sally said, 'absolutely great. Oh, here's Lachie and Angus.

How does it feel to be famous, Angus?'

Angus's colour heightened, though he had listened to Sally's teasing for years.

'I wouldn't know.' He grinned. 'How about becoming famous and telling me?'

'But you're going off to Brazil to paint!'

'I shall bring home a nut, specially for you.' Angus said, tweaking her nose amidst general laughter.

It was a lovely party, and one which Kate was to remember for a long time. Her stepmother's lovely supper set the tone for the evening, and her eyes glowed as she and Gavin Reid relived the happy days of their honeymoon, while Keith showed the slides they had taken.

'I loved the shops.' Caroline Reid said rather wistfully.

There had been no thought, then, of the economies she would now have to make, though they had put all that behind them tonight.

Later, Angus came to stand beside Kate, and for a long moment their eyes met and held.

Her heart bounded with a surge of feeling for him, then suddenly Lachie came up behind her, laughing as he turned to both of them.

Gavin Reid had just made a small speech, wishing Angus well and hoping for great success in Brazil.

'We'll have just as exciting a time here at home, won't we, Kate?' said Lachie.

'You know. Angus, this commission of yours has made me realise how quietly we live here in Stronmore, but I intend to change that a bit after you go.

'I intend that Kate and I will have a good time. Won't we, Kate?'

Again Kate's eyes met Angus's, and she quickly looked away. Moira Johnstone had heard Lachie's remark, and the light dimmed in the girl's eyes. She had been discussing books with Keith and now she turned away as he found one for her to borrow.

'I want to go to bed. Auntie Kate,' said Norrie firmly, tugging at her dress.

'All right, pet. Let's go.' Kate said, taking his hand.

She walked quietly away, leading the child, though inwardly she felt upset and disturbed. Angus must have his chance. She must feel delighted for him to be going to Brazil, even if it led to other commissions and more travel abroad.

In spite of Sally's teasing, Angus might very well be famous some day, and he deserved all his success. But how she would miss him! And how difficult it was going to be not to upset Lachie or hurt Moira.

Keith had been very nice to the young girl this evening, hovering around with paying her attention, but it was Lachie who drew her eyes.

⋆   ⋆   ⋆

Over the next week or two they saw little of Angus at Hazelbank. Kate had expected Sally to go back to London after the party, but she informed them she had a few days' holiday, and once or twice Kate had found her at the phone, though the receiver was quickly replaced.

'Don't mind me,' Kate said, not above hovering around to see if she could get some sort of insight into Sally's problems.

'We've all got to cut down, haven't we?' Sally asked in her usual defiant tones. 'I'm just being careful over the bills. You can't have it both ways.'

Towards the end of the week she received a letter and announced that she would be staying at home for one more week. Kate eyed her levelly.

'Well, cheer up then, and try to help Caroline a bit more. We can't afford to have Molly Simpson more than two days a week now, and she's helping Dr Spiers in between times. But it means a lot of work for Caroline.'

Caroline was feeling the strain in the aftermath of the family party, and she was worrying a little about Gavin.

'I don't like the way Angus seems to be spending so much time at work,' he told her. 'Maybe I'm just learning to be suspicious of the two boys, but I can't help feeling they're still keeping something from me, so I'm going over there to investigate, Caroline.'

'Well, go easy, then, darling,' she said. 'You know, I don't think you realise just how long it takes to get back to full strength after the sort of operation you've had. I don't like to keep harping on . . . '

'I promise to let up as soon as I feel tired,' he said. 'But it does more harm than good to be sitting here worrying myself.'

'That's true,' his wife conceded.

Gavin had found Angus deep in plans for the work at West Lodge, though he had been about to leave for the site.

'I'll come with you,' Gavin Reid said easily.

Angus hesitated. 'Well, it isn't so important,' he hedged.

'Good. We'll talk on the way,' Gavin assured him firmly.

It didn't take long for Mr Reid to weigh up the work being done on the old house, and his eyes immediately went to the panelling which was being renovated. There was a great deal more of it than he had thought.

'Who's doing this?' he asked Angus. 'Tom Andrews used to do panelling, but he's away now, isn't he?'

Angus nodded. 'We never really replaced Tom, though Bob Simpson can manage simple repairs. I had a go at this myself.'

Gavin Reid frowned, then went to examine the intricate panelling, his respect for Angus increasing tenfold, though he had always known Angus could carve.

'Why didn't you tell me?' he asked. 'You can't be expected to do this yourself, Angus.'

Gavin pursed his lips, quickly assessing how much was still to be done.

'There is so little time before I go,'

196

Angus continued. 'This commission has come just at the wrong time.'

'No, it's the *right* time.' Gavin Reid disagreed. 'And it's the right time for me, too. I'm coming back to work tomorrow, Angus.'

'But you can't!' cried Angus. 'It's hard work.'

'I know how hard it is, lad. I haven't forgotten! But I'm going to do it just the same. I rather think I'm going to enjoy it.'

Angus smiled at the older man uncertainly. It would be a great relief to him, but he had noticed how quickly Mr Reid could become tired nowadays compared with what he used to be like.

'We could maybe work together,' he offered, 'so that the job would be done more quickly. The rest of it is fairly straightforward, but we need the money for all this intricate work, Mr Reid.'

'I know, and I'm very grateful, Angus. But you've got yourself an assistant.'

Keith heard the news that his stepfather was coming back to work with mixed feelings. He was getting used to his responsibilities now, and Angus and he had formed a fine partnership.

He enjoyed the companionable way they could work things out.

How would he get on after Gavin Reid came back to take charge once again, he wondered, as they all sat round the table for supper that evening.

Kate had been rather quiet over the past few days, and it seemed to Keith that she was worrying herself over something.

He looked at the younger girl, who seemed to do little else but loaf around the house most of the day.

He had heard Kate admonishing Sally and telling her to help his mother, but it seemed to go in one ear and out the other.

Keith bit his lip, thinking how happy he had been after Mr Reid found out about his problems over the business.

It had been a relief to get it all off his chest, and his spirits had soared so that his heart was light with happiness. He had even had time to take an interest in friends again, and had taken a great liking to Moira Johnstone.

But now things were going wrong again, and some of his lightness of heart drained away. Moodily, he sat in the lounge while his mother and Kate washed up in the kitchen and Gavin Reid went off to his study.

Sally had spread herself along the full length of the settee, propping up a magazine.

'Why aren't you helping in the kitchen?' Keith asked, exasperated by her.

Sally stared at him over the magazine.

'Why aren't you?' she countered.

'At least I've put in a good day's work,' he replied heatedly.

'So has Kate!'

'And my mother! Yet all you do is

slouch around here all day . . . '

'What do you know about it?' cried Sally hysterically. 'You know nothing about my feelings.'

'We all have feelings,' shouted Keith, his own nerves frayed. 'Why should we all have to consider yours?'

'Keith! That's enough!'

They looked round to see Caroline Reid standing in the doorway.

# Under Suspicion

Caroline Reid's cheeks were flushed as she looked at her son and stepdaughter. Keith's eyes sparkled with anger and his mother came over to stand beside him.

'I don't want to hear any more, Keith,' she said quietly. 'I know it isn't easy for two families to settle down happily together, but we've got to try — and we're going to succeed! Let's have no more of this stupid behaviour!'

Keith bit his lip, then slowly nodded. He turned to look at Sally, but Caroline Reid had rounded on her, also.

'That goes for you, too, Sally,' she said clearly. 'We all have to give and take a little and show a bit more consideration for one another, and you're not without blame. Keith has a point, you know. You could help a little more, if you tried.'

Sally stared at her stepmother, her bottom lip beginning to tremble, then she rushed from the room, pushing past Kate on her way to the stairs.

The noise of her pounding footsteps brought her father out of his study, and he looked up at her hurrying figure, then walked slowly into the lounge to join the other members of the family.

'What's going on?' Gavin Reid asked.

'Oh, just family squabbles,' his wife replied brightly.

'What sort of family squabbles?' Gavin Reid was asking.

'My fault, I'm afraid,' Keith said ruefully, turning to smile at his stepfather. 'I had a difference of opinion with Sally and Mother has straightened us out . . . both of us!' he added. 'I'd better go and apologise, and make my peace with Sally.'

'I see,' said Gavin Reid, though his eyes went once again to the stairs. 'I — I've got one or two things still to attend to, my dear,' he said, turning to

Caroline. 'I'll come through for coffee later.'

'Very well, darling.' Caroline Reid said.

Her husband had accepted her explanation, but he had obviously still been uneasy. She sighed, thinking that it was going to take some time yet to bring them all together as one family.

The following morning was almost like old times, thought Kate, as her father hurried downstairs for breakfast, clad in his workday clothes.

Keith had risen earlier and had already left for the workshop.

He had made his peace with Sally, who was still sulking a little, though she had joined the family for a light supper the previous evening before going to bed.

Together they had all watched a late-night television programme, but Sally had been very subdued, and her father had looked at her reflectively, more than once.

Keith had brought her the plate of

sandwiches and had smiled when he offered them to her, and Sally smiled a little as she took one.

Caroline Reid had relaxed a little, feeling that the family relationships were better than she had hoped, though she couldn't help worrying about Sally. There was something here which she just could not understand.

Keith, on the other hand, had dismissed Sally completely from his mind as he went over all the papers on his desk. He was uneasy about a new consignment of wood, though Angus had inspected it and thought it was the same as usual.

However, the years spent in the large timber yard where he had been employed before joining the company had developed in Keith a strange extra sense for the feel of wood, and he didn't think that the consignment was quite up to standard.

'It seems OK to me,' Angus said, picking up one of the planks and running his hands over it. 'It isn't easy to get really good wood these days. There's always such a need for a quick turnover.'

'I know,' Keith agreed rather unhappily.

★   ★   ★

When Gavin Reid arrived half an hour later to discuss the work schedule, he nodded to Keith then turned to Angus, and for a long moment Keith watched as the two men pored over plans.

He knew his stepfather would be going with Angus out to West Lodge, where he would begin to help with the intricate panelling.

'The new wood has come,' Angus said, 'though Keith is a bit uncertain about it.'

'Oh, what's up with it, Keith?' Gavin asked.

'Just . . . just something about the feel of it,' Keith said rather uncomfortably. 'It looks OK, though, and it has been tested. Maybe we'd better just forget it. My imagination is working overtime.'

'The wood seems all right to me, Mr Reid,' Angus said, and the older man nodded after pausing thoughtfully.

'Oh well, let's get over to West Lodge, Angus,' he said briskly. 'The quicker we get on with that panelling, the better. See you later, Keith.'

Keith nodded and turned back to a pile of correspondence on his desk. He would be able to deal with quite a lot of it, though the first invoice he picked up was for the new consignment of wood.

Keith stood for a long moment debating with himself, then went to find Bob Simpson. It would do no harm just to make another test on that plank of wood, on his own initiative.

Bob Simpson was hard at work, but he smiled broadly as Keith came over.

'I see the boss is back in harness,' he remarked. 'It's nice to see Mr Reid back again.'

'It certainly is,' Keith agreed, then handed Bob the plank of wood, going into technical details about the tests he wanted carried out.

'Maybe I'm a fusspot, Bob,' he finished, 'but this will just make sure.'

'You've a real feel for wood, Mr Drummond,' Bob said, 'and that reminds me, you asked if I could make you a wee trinket box from small off-cuts, didn't you?'

Keith blushed. Moira Johnstone's birthday was soon and Keith had thought that she would like an unusual trinket box as a present.

'Well . . . only if you had time, Bob,' he said rather awkwardly.

'What about this idea?' Bob asked, producing a beautiful box made up of small squares of walnut, sycamore and mahogany. It had been polished to mirror brightness.

'It's really beautiful,' Keith said, running his hands over the lovely little box, then he insisted on paying Bob for all the care he had taken.

★   ★   ★

On Thursday evening Keith arranged to leave work early to go over to Meadowpark and see Moira.

At the young girl's insistence, her birthday had been celebrated very quietly, though Gemma had made a special cake for tea.

She was now resting most of the day, and depending a great deal on Moira, but it had taken more patience than effort to make the birthday cake.

Besides Moira's own family, Kate and Keith had remembered her birthday. Both had visited the farm one evening when Gemma had laughingly told their fortunes from the stars, and they had remembered the birthday date Moira had given.

When Keith called later in the evening, Norrie was wearing a paper hat, and his cheeks were covered in jam and cake crumbs.

'Auntie Moira is having a birthday party,' he informed Keith excitedly. 'She's got ten candles on her cake.'

'It was all I could find.' Gemma

laughed and insisted that Keith pull in his chair and try a piece of cake.

'Norrie's getting too excited,' she said. 'He's been allowed to stay up too late.'

Shyly Moira was opening her present and her cheeks glowed with excitement and a hint of embarrassment when she saw the pretty box.

'Oh, Keith! You shouldn't have!'

'I got Bob Simpson to make it for me. I thought you might like it.'

'I do, but . . . ' She broke off, then nodded her acceptance. 'I love it. Thank you very much, Keith. Now I'd better take this young man up to bed.'

'I'll help you,' Keith offered, and again Moira hesitated, though Norrie soon made the decision for her.

'I want Uncle Keith to carry me,' he announced, and the two girls were happy to see him climbing the stairs without protest.

It was while Keith was reading a story to Norman, after tucking him up in bed, that the bell rang and Moira went to open the door.

Keith could hear Lachie's deep voice, then Moira's, as she directed him towards the barn.

'Alec's not too happy about one of the calves,' she explained. 'He's just been ringing the vet.'

'Oh, I'd better have a word with him,' Lachie said. 'Actually he wanted to borrow some tools. I've brought them over.'

'Would you care to look in for a cup of tea and a slice of cake after you've finished with Alec?' Moira asked.

'I wouldn't mind a cup of tea,' Lachie agreed.

Moira smiled. 'See you later, then, Lachie.'

But it was almost an hour later before Lachie and Alec had finished all they wanted to discuss in the barn.

The vet arrived and Lachie wanted to see if he was needed in helping with the sick calf. He and Alec were both tired when the calf was eventually made comfortable and they walked towards the farmhouse kitchen door.

'Moira asked me to call in for a cup of tea,' Lachie explained.

'Oh, of course,' said Alec. 'It's her birthday today.'

'I . . . I didn't know,' Lachie said.

He was looking at a car which was parked at the back of the house.

'Isn't that Keith Drummond's car?' he asked, but before Alec could answer, Keith himself appeared from the direction of the house, whistling cheerily.

'Hello, Lachie,' he called. 'Isn't it a fine night?'

'You seem very pleased with yourself,' Lachie commented.

Keith laughed, colouring a little. 'I've just been to see Moira,' he said. 'Helping her celebrate her birthday.'

'I didn't know about that,' Lachie repeated, feeling strangely put out.

'Well . . . good night then,' Keith said, turning to smile at Alec. 'I hope the calf is OK.'

'So do I,' Alec said. 'Good night, Keith.'

Lachie looked after him as he drove away, then he followed Alec into the house.

The following evening Lachie called in to see Kate and found her busy cutting out a new dress.

'I thought you might like to have gone to the pictures in Tordale,' he said, disappointed.

'I'm sorry, Lachie,' she said, looking up with flushed cheeks as she changed the pattern round to save material. 'I'm trying to make this dress in time for the badminton club social and dance.'

'Oh, yes.' Lachie nodded. 'I heard Angus mention it. We're all hoping to go.'

'It will probably be the last social event before Angus leaves for Brazil.'

Lachie glanced at her keenly. But Kate was shaking her head ruefully over her pattern.

'I think I'm going to have to call on Caroline for help,' she confessed, 'after she's stopped fussing over Dad. He started work this week, and she insists that he has a good rest in the evenings.

'How about helping me to make some supper. Lachie, and we'll carry it into the lounge and call everybody.'

'Done.' Lachie said. 'Where do I start?'

'You put the kettle on.' Kate laughed.

Ten minutes later, supper was ready. Lachie carried the tray through to the lounge where only Sally was sitting reading.

Lachie turned to look at Sally.

'Are you still on holiday, Sal?' he asked. 'Or are you stuck for a job?'

Sally coloured brightly.

'Honestly, you'd think I'd been home for weeks,' she protested. 'I'm not stuck for a job and it isn't your business anyway, Lachie Fraser.'

'Sorry!' he cried, holding up his arms to ward off imaginary blows.

Kate was looking at her sister. In spite of Sally's words, she had been at home a long time and there had been a note almost of fear in her voice when she mentioned her job.

★ ★ ★

Later, Kate made sure Sally had gone up to bed before her, then she knocked lightly on her bedroom door and slipped into the room.

'You're late up tonight,' she remarked to Kate. 'I thought you had to get up for work in the morning.'

'I do, but I had to unpin my dress pattern. Caroline is going to try it for me tomorrow.'

Kate came over and sat down on her sister's bed.

'Will you be here for the dance. Sally?' she asked.

Sally seemed to withdraw a little.

'Why?'

'Oh, I just wondered whether or not your holiday would be over. You've been given quite a lot of time off, haven't you?'

'Why shouldn't I?' Sally demanded,

flags of colour in her cheeks. 'I've worked for it.'

'Have you? You never say very much about your job, do you? You never talk about it. Working in a hotel is not really top secret, is it?'

'If I did talk about it all the time, you'd be asking me to give it a rest. You'd all be bored to death. There's no pleasing you. Kate. You grumble when I don't come home, then grumble when my holiday lasts longer than two weeks. If I'm in the way ...'

'You know it isn't that.' Kate said swiftly. 'I like having you home, but ... but I can't help feeling that you're worried about something.'

'I've told you. I'm OK.'

Kate sighed and stood up. She was now even more certain that Sally was far from OK and it was all the more disquieting when she refused to talk about it.

She had never had to force Sally's confidence in the past, and now she didn't quite know how to handle her sister.

'All right, Sally,' she said and dropped a light kiss on her young sister's fair curls. 'Good night. See you in the morning.'

''Night,' mumbled Sally, 'and, Kate — thanks for everything.'

★   ★   ★

The following morning Sally hadn't appeared for breakfast before Kate left for work, and when Caroline Reid returned in the late morning after a shopping spree, she still hadn't come down from the bedroom.

Surely the girl hadn't stayed in bed until this time? Perhaps she had overslept.

She went upstairs hurriedly and tapped on Sally's door. There was no reply, so she pushed it open and peered in. The girl was sound asleep and the bedclothes showed signs of a very restless night.

Caroline Reid walked slowly towards the bed, seeing signs of tears on the young girl's cheeks, which were warm and flushed. Perhaps she wasn't feeling well. She put a hand on Sally's forehead.

Sally's eyes opened and stared at Caroline.

'I . . . I just wondered if you were all right,' her stepmother said awkwardly. 'You haven't come down for breakfast. Stay there, dear, and I'll make something for you.'

Sally said nothing. Her head was aching after a restless night and now she gasped a little when she saw the time.

'I'll get up,' she called to her stepmother.

'No, stay there, dear. I'll be back in a minute or two with some breakfast.'

Tired, Sally lay back until Caroline appeared with a tray of coffee and toast and her thermometer.

'Pop this in your mouth before you have that coffee,' she commanded.

'No. really, I . . . I'm fine.' Sally said, then found it difficult to speak when her stepmother put the thermometer under her tongue.

'Hm . . . yes, your temperature is normal,' she agreed, looking at the thermometer.

'I told you. I . . . I just slept in, that's all. Thanks for the breakfast, though, Caroline.'

Caroline pulled up a chair and sat down as she handed Sally the toast.

'Well, if it isn't flu, what is it?' she asked. 'You can't tell me a girl of your age would spend such a sleepless night for nothing. I don't want to pry, dear, but I am your stepmother, and I feel responsible for you.

'Is it boyfriend trouble? Oddly enough, I had some of that myself when I was your age. It wasn't always the end of the world, but it felt like it.'

Sally smiled a little.

'No, I haven't got boyfriend trouble,' she said. 'No, it isn't anything like that.'

'What is it then?' Caroline Reid asked.

Sally's cheeks had grown scarlet and she bit her lip, annoyed that she had admitted to having a problem.

'It's nothing . . . nothing I can't handle,' she said huskily. 'It's sure to come right in the end. It must!'

'I think you'd better tell me.' Her stepmother was quietly persistent.

For a long time Sally sipped her coffee while Caroline waited.

'I . . . I was busy at the time.' Sally said eventually in a low voice. 'I was on duty at the reception desk of the hotel where I work — you know all about that, don't you?'

Caroline noddded and Sally drew a deep breath.

'It was just at our busiest time with the phone ringing and . . . and all that sort of thing.

'Mrs Naismith, one of our guests, asked me to lock away some of her valuables. We have to write the items down in a book and Mrs Naismith had to sign that it was correct. She was reading out the descriptions of all the items while I wrote them down . . . '

'All right, dear, just take it quietly. What happened then?'

'The phone kept on ringing,' Sally said, 'and I picked it up and I had to write down a message. I forgot to count the valuable items from Mrs Naismith and check them against the list.

'Later, when she got them back, a gold pin with pearls and a turquoise was missing.

'She wore it at a ball in the hotel the previous evening and there was a photographer taking pictures. She has a copy of the photograph, so we know she had the pin . . . '

Sally's voice was trembling and her eyes were brimming with tears. Caroline Reid gathered her into her arms.

'I just don't remember it,' Sally said, her body shaking with sobs, 'yet it must have been there.

'Mrs Naismith has been coming to the hotel for years. She . . . she just isn't the sort of lady who would say she had lost her brooch when she hadn't. She'd never involve me in any trouble unless she really had lost the brooch, if . . . if you know what I mean.'

'I know what you mean,' Caroline Reid nodded. 'You feel she's an honest woman.'

'Yes. But the brooch is valuable and when Mrs Naismith tried to claim on her insurance, they said the police must be brought in. I've been suspended until enquiries are made . . . '

Sally's voice tailed off and she sobbed quietly in her stepmother's arms. Even as she stroked her hair, she began to feel the great pressing weight lift a little.

'There, darling, have a good cry. It will help,' she said.

'I . . . I don't know what's going to happen now, but thank you. Caroline. I feel better,' Sally said at last.

Caroline Reid brushed Sally's soft curls from her forehead.

'It will all come right, don't you worry,' she said encouragingly.

But, as she walked downstairs, her brows wrinkled a little with worry. Suppose the gold pin didn't turn up, how would her husband take this news?

Caroline Reid asked Sally to help her with ideas for Kate's new dress. It kept Sally occupied, and together they managed to make the sort of dress Kate had often dreamed of.

Angus had asked Kate to go with him as his partner, and after a momentary look of disappointment. Lachie had shrugged and appeared disappointed.

'I thought we were all going as a crowd,' he suggested.

'Of course we are.' Angus grinned. 'I'm just making sure of dancing with Kate!'

Moira was also excitedly looking forward to the dance.

Over the past few days Sally had become much more sociable and she had gone over to Meadowpark to look after Norrie while Moira and Gemma had a quiet day in Tordale.

The family had given Sally their quiet

sympathy and staunch support when she finally told them about her trouble in London.

Her father had hugged her and insisted on hearing every detail, then he had decided that they should wait and see what happened.

Only his wife knew how deeply disturbed he was by what he had heard, and she found herself worrying again about his health.

★   ★   ★

The night of the dance, however, found a very different atmosphere in the house as the young people all dressed up for the evening.

Instinctively, Sally felt it was Kate's evening and she had chosen a plain, simple dress in palest blue which, to her surprise, made her look more beautiful than anything else she could have possibly chosen to wear.

Sally spent most of her time helping her stepmother to arrange Kate's new dress, which swirled in soft golden folds to her feet. Kate's small, slim figure had never looked more elegant, and her dark hair shone like a halo round her head.

Kate enjoyed herself thoroughly, as she danced with Angus, then with Lachie and then with Keith.

'Will you have dinner with me tomorrow evening?' Angus asked quickly before she was whirled away by yet another partner.

Kate's eyes shone.

'All right, Angus,' she agreed, and hugged the thought of the invitation to her heart as they all drove home, and tiptoed up to bed.

The following morning all three were downstairs rather late while Caroline and Gavin Reid smiled at their sleepy faces.

'I think I must have danced every dance,' said Keith, and his mother smiled happily.

'Lachie has big feet,' Sally grumbled, 'and he has no sense of rhythm.'

'You've got to allow for that!' Kate laughed. 'What he lacks in technique, he makes up for with enthusiasm. Lachie enjoys himself.'

'So does Angus,' Sally said roguishly. 'And, speak of the devil, I think he's about to pay us a visit. He has just passed the window in a tearing hurry.'

'Oh,' Kate said, turning towards the door.

A moment later, Angus had rushed in.

'Hello, Angus,' cried Sally. 'You look as though you've got a mad dog after you.'

'Just about,' Angus agreed, looking round hurriedly as Kate came towards him.

'I . . . I'm sorry, Kate,' he told her breathlessly, 'but I'll have to break our date for tonight. I've just had a call from the chemical corporation and I must catch the train to London straightaway. I'll have to make a dash for it. It's a very important meeting and I've just got to be there. There's just no time, Kate.'

He looked at her again, then squeezed her fingers tightly.

'I'm so sorry I've got to rush like this, but I'll be in touch as soon as I get to Brazil, I promise.'

He gave Kate a brief hug and was on his way, scarcely hearing Kate's quiet goodbye. She came to the door and watched him get into the car and drive off.

Even with the promise of letters to come, six weeks was going to be a long time without Angus, and when he did return, would her feelings for him be the same?

# The Beautiful Stranger

It seemed to Kate that a lifetime had passed before she turned to go back indoors after watching Angus drive away.

There was a sick, empty feeling of disappointment in her heart, and for a long moment she stood outside, trying to get her bearings before facing the family.

They mustn't see her heartache. They already had enough worry about getting the company back on its feet — especially now that Angus had gone.

Kate slowly walked back through the kitchen door and sat down again at the breakfast table.

'Well,' she said brightly, 'that's Angus away now. I could have done with being a label on his luggage! It must be a wonderful trip for him. I — I don't think I've ever seen him so excited.'

She turned to find Sally looking at her closely, then turning away when she found Caroline's eyes on her.

There had been sympathy on Caroline's face, and Kate felt the hard lump in her throat beginning to dissolve into tears. She was going to miss Angus very much. Her father had risen, excusing himself from the table, to do some work in his study, and Caroline had gone to the phone.

'Is it my turn to wash up?' Keith asked. Sally laughed at the doleful note in his voice.

'I know how you feel, Keith,' she said, 'but if you've got better things to do, I'll do it for you. But you'll owe me a job, mind! You don't get off so easily.'

'Take her temperature,' Keith said to Kate. 'She can't be feeling well to make such an offer!'

'You'd better go, then, before I recover,' Sally told him.

Both laughed. Since their row they had bickered but in a much more amiable way. Kate quietly stacked the breakfast dishes, deciding she would wash up. She needed something to do.

'You can stop arguing,' she said. 'I'll do it.'

'We both will,' said Sally, and Kate was glad to listen to her meaningless chatter as she dried the dishes and put them away.

'How about us going into Tordale to the pictures this evening?' Sally suggested.

'Oh, I don't think so ... ' Kate began. She was in no mood to go to the cinema.

'It's ages since we went out together, just the two of us,' Sally coaxed.

Kate paused, thinking that at one time Sally would have considered going around with her sister very dull. She was trying to be kind, thought Kate, as she rinsed her dishcloth.

'That might not be such a bad idea, Sally,' she said slowly, blinking back a tear which unfortunately rolled down her cheek. Sally squeezed her hand and then quietly handed her a tissue.

★ ★ ★

On Monday morning Keith found things more than usually chaotic when he went over to the workshop.

Gavin Reid had decided to go straight over to West Lodge, where the work was proceeding satisfactorily. He felt he couldn't afford to waste a minute now he no longer had Angus's help.

'Will you manage without me over at the workshop?' he asked Keith that morning. Normally he and Angus got through quite a lot of paperwork before starting their practical jobs.

'Sure,' Keith said, more confidently than he felt.

Already a number of queries had built up, and Keith was aware that the men were standing about, a little uncertain as to what was to happen, and he squared his shoulders. Maybe he wasn't as competent as Angus at dealing with problems, but he intended to try.

'We'll just go through and see these then, Bob,' he said to Bob Simpson, picking up the time sheets. 'Most things seem to be straightforward.'

Crisply he gave his orders, and fought down any misgivings he had as to whether or not he was making the right decisions.

In the late afternoon Bob Simpson came to find Keith, carrying a piece of wood which had been subjected to rigorous testing. Bob's kindly face wore a look of concern, mingled with respect.

'You were right about this wood, Keith,' he said, coming straight to the point. 'It is certainly not up to usual standards. I wouldn't give it very long before it started to warp.'

'Let me see,' Keith said, examining it all carefully. 'I had a feeling about that wood. I'd better get on to the supplier.'

'We've got our problems now, Keith. Where are we going to get the wood we need?'

'Leave that to me. Bob,' said Keith

confidently. In this field he was on sure ground. He was positive that, left to himself, he could find another supplier.

'Yes, but it isn't only that, Keith. Mr Reid has been using this wood at West Lodge.'

Keith sat down and stared hard at Bob.

'Has there been much of it used?'

'Quite a lot. It looks as though it'll all have to be done again.'

Keith's supple fingers ran over the faulty wood.

'I'd better go over to West Lodge,' he said, looking at his watch. 'The quicker Mr Reid knows about this, the better.'

West Lodge was beginning to look very different from the old neglected house which Mr Richmond had bought.

Keith paused for a moment as he walked into the large hall, feeling a sense of pride that he was part of the firm which had done such a wonderful job of the restoration.

There couldn't be many firms in the

country, he thought, capable of carrying out such skilled work. The new carved panelling fitted in with such precision and perfection that it was difficult to see which parts had been replaced.

The air of neglect had now gone, and every room seemed to glow with the loving care which had gone into it.

Keith walked through into the library, where a large section of panelling required to be replaced. His stepfather was busy planing a piece of new wood, and he looked up, rather startled, when he saw Keith walking in.

'Hello, Keith,' he called. 'What brings you out here?' His voice suddenly sharpened. 'Is everything all right? At home, I mean?'

'Fine,' said Keith. 'I thought I'd better come to see you, though. Would you like to have a look at this piece of wood?'

Soon he was going into details about the tests he'd carried out on the new wood, and Gavin's face was grave as he looked at the results, turning the wood over in his hands.

'It would be all right for normal purposes, but certainly not for West Lodge,' he agreed. 'You were right after all, Keith.'

'I thought that some new methods had been used on it, and I don't think you can take short-cuts like that with this particular type of wood. We need something that will stand the test of time.'

Gavin Reid was looking at his stepson with respect as well as affection.

'I . . . I just can't say how grateful I am, Keith,' he said steadily. 'It's bad enough as things stand now, but if we had finished the job — well, I hardly need to tell you.' He sat down, staring round the room.

'Have you used much of it?' Keith asked.

Gavin Reid nodded. 'Too much for my liking. It looks as though a great deal of work will have to be done again, this time without Angus.'

They looked at one another silently

for a while, then Mr Reid sighed.

'Never mind. We'll manage it somehow. Do you think you can get us some other wood? And we'll certainly have to see what the suppliers say about this consignment.'

'I'll deal with them,' Keith assured him. 'And I'll get you some wood, never fear.'

'Good lad,' Gavin Reid said simply, and Keith felt the pressure of his stepfather's fingers on his shoulder.

* * *

Keith was late leaving the workshop that evening, and as he walked across to Hazelbank, Lachie's pick-up drew up beside him.

'Like a lift?' Lachie grinned.

'What? Ten yards? I'm not in my dotage yet!'

'I only wanted to tell you that we've seen Angus on the news. Obviously you'll have missed it.'

'I expect we've all missed it,' said

Keith ruefully. 'We usually watch the later news. I wonder if it will be repeated.'

'I expect it will,' said Lachie. 'There seems to be quite a party going to Brazil.'

'I'll go and tell the family then,' Keith said. 'I'm sure they'll want to see Angus on TV — especially Kate.'

'Er — yes,' said Lachie, rather hesitantly. 'As I say, it's probably a working party because there were other people with him. This new development in Brazil seems to be very big and modern.'

'We'll be very interested,' Keith said, waving to Lachie as he drove away.

Kate was excited when Keith gave them all the news around the dinner table.

'We'd better not go to badminton then,' said Sally. 'I've been coaxing Kate to go with me, and we'd planned to ask you, too, Keith. You could do with a bit of exercise. You're getting too fat.'

Mr and Mrs Reid turned to grin at

one another. Keith had a long way to go before anyone considered him fat!

'You'll be sorry when I do go to play,' Keith returned. 'I'll beat you with one hand tied behind my back. What about Moira? Wouldn't she like to join?'

'We can always ask her,' Kate said.

At nine o'clock the family gathered round the television set, waiting excitedly while other items of news were dealt with.

Towards the end of the bulletin, the news reader turned to a new industrial complex that had just been opened in Brazil, and to the work which Angus had been commissioned to do. The Managing Director had been interviewed, along with Angus, and now scenes were shown in the large modern plant.

'A great deal of land must have been cleared,' the interviewer said, 'in order to build this plant. Doesn't that affect the environment, Mr Bailey?'

'No indeed,' explained Mr Bailey. 'We have commissioned Angus Fraser to paint pictures of the wildlife here, and we intend to hold an exhibition of these paintings in London later in the year, together with photographs, which will show the care taken to preserve all aspects of the environment.

'In fact, our chemicals can often be employed in saving wildlife instead of destroying it, as some people imagine.'

Then the cameras were on Angus, and Kate's heart leapt to see his familiar smile on the screen; for a long moment he seemed to be looking at only her.

'Your pictures are already well known, Mr Fraser,' the interviewer said, as examples of Angus's work were shown on the screen. 'Can you give us some idea of what you intend to paint?'

'Perhaps I ought to wait till I get there.' Angus smiled. 'I'm sure I'll have plenty of choice.'

The cameras turned to a third member of the team, who was introduced as Miss Felicity Powers, daughter of the chairman of the company.

'Will Miss Powers feature in the paintings?' the interviewer asked, and Kate watched the ready colour rushing into Angus's cheeks as they all laughed.

Angus had never mentioned this girl, though she was not the sort of girl you could overlook.

'I'm joining my father in Brazil,' Miss Powers said huskily. 'There is still a great deal of work to be done. I'm a photographer.' And she smiled at the reporter.

The cameras cut to the team boarding the plane and Kate watched Angus turn to smile at Felicity Powers as they boarded the plane together.

She felt as though her heart was turning to ice. The family were laughing happily, commenting on the fact that Angus was becoming quite a celebrity, but Kate scarcely heard them.

She knew now that it was Angus she loved.

But what did Angus feel for her? Did he love her as someone she had known all his life? Was his love for her the warmth of a long, close association, rather than the true love she felt for him?

Long after the news had finished, Kate could once again see Angus's smiling eyes as he turned to look at Felicity Powers. How beautiful the girl was — almost as tall as Angus — with lovely, stylish clothes.

Kate felt herself insignificant beside the other girl. She couldn't blame Angus if he fell for her.

'Here! A cup of coffee,' Sally said, by her side. 'Cheer up! He'll soon be back home again. Why don't you go and ring Lachie and tell him we've seen the news?'

Kate pulled herself together.

'Thanks, Sally,' she said and managed a quick smile. 'I think I'll do that.'

★   ★   ★

Lachie put down the phone after Kate had rung. This should have been a happy moment for him, but in an odd way he felt far from being at peace with

240

himself. He had agreed to go down to Hazelbank the following evening and join the young people who were going to the badminton club.

He would be Kate's partner and would no doubt spend a great deal of the evening in her company.

Over the past few weeks he had been gradually facing up to the fact that Kate loved Angus and not him, even if she didn't know it herself.

He had watched her eyes sometimes, as they rested on Angus, and with deep insight, he felt he had seen into her heart. Kate wasn't for him, thought Lachie, and he might as well face up to that fact.

But now he was finding his thoughts straying more and more in the direction of Meadowpark, and instead of seeing Kate's dark eyes, he was visualising Moira Johnstone and remembering how her eyes would light up when she came to answer the door.

Yet Keith Drummond also kept going over to Meadowpark to see

Moira, and Keith showed all too clearly that he found her very attractive. Was Moira equally friendly with Keith, he wondered, surprising himself by the jealousy this aroused in him.

He was used to looking his problems straight in the face, and the more he thought about Moira, the more determined he became to go all out to make himself important to her.

He wasn't going to stand idly by while Keith walked off with her. Moira was a girl worth fighting for.

There was a surge of excitement in him as he walked down to Hazelbank the following evening to pick up Kate and Sally on the way to the badminton club.

'Keith has gone up to Meadowpark,' Kate said brightly, 'to pick up Moira. He's determined to beat us this evening, so you'll have to partner me, Lachie, and give more strength to my elbow.'

Lachie stared at her. If she was missing Angus she gave no sign, nor did it appear to worry her that he would be working in close contact with Felicity Powers. But then, Kate always liked to fight her own battles.

'Keith and Moira have no chance against us,' he said firmly. 'But I hope we can change partners, too ... you and Keith against Moira and me. Sally, too — though she's good enough to beat us all single handed.'

'Oh, I shan't be playing much,' Sally said rather listlessly. She had been a great deal less worried after telling the family about her troubles in London, but that phase had passed now, and her fears were growing again.

Her problems were far from resolved, and she was beginning to sleep badly. At one time she would have retreated into herself, but watching Kate going about normally when underneath she was eating her heart out for Angus Fraser, had made Sally pull herself together and realise others had worries.

Kate had never pushed her problems on to someone else, and Sally was determined to try to behave in the same sort of way. But although she had decided to go to the badminton club rather than stay in and mope, she didn't feel energetic enough to play many games.

Moira Johnstone looked very fit as she and Keith beat Kate and Lachie well and truly. The good fresh farm air had brought colour to Moira's cheeks and a sparkle to her eyes, and she so obviously enjoyed Keith's light-hearted banter. She had grown into a very attractive girl, thought Kate, as she looked at Moira's shining eyes.

Lachie also watched them, thinking how much he liked Moira, and how easy she was to talk to. Perhaps he had shown her all too clearly that he had been interested only in Kate. Perhaps she thought there could never be anything serious between them. Yet he was sure she had liked him when they first met.

'I think we could change partners now,' he said, grinning as he met

Keith's eyes. 'We'll see how well matched Moira and I are.'

Keith hesitated, and Kate hid a smile as she saw how competently Lachie arranged things so that he got Moira on his side.

It was Moira and Lachie who beat Keith and Kate, and the younger girl smiled happily at both young men. She had grown up, thought Kate.

Sally had decided to go home early, pleading a headache, and Keith lost no time in offering to take Moira home.

Lachie nodded, though he smiled warmly as he bade Moira good night, and promised to call at Meadowpark the following day.

'I hope you're in a mood to walk,' he said, as he turned to Kate. 'I'd better remind you that I didn't bring the pick-up.'

'It's a nice evening,' Kate said. 'Of course we'll walk.'

They set out as they had done so often in the past, with Lachie slowing his pace to suit Kate.

'I wonder what Angus is doing at this moment,' he mused.

'Whatever it is, it's sure to be exciting,' Kate said evenly, her voice betraying nothing.

That morning she had brought in the post, her heart leaping when she saw the airmail letter in Angus's strong, bold handwriting.

She had slipped it into her pocket deciding to read it when she was alone.

But the letter had told her very little. It was just a quick note to reassure her that all was well, and that he would write more fully when he arrived in Brazil.

He made no mention of Felicity Powers, and Kate bit her lip because of that omission.

Again and again she saw Angus's face as he turned to smile at the lovely girl, and tried to fight down her own feelings. She only wanted Angus to be happy, and he must be free to live his own life as he wanted to.

'You're very quiet,' she said to Lachie.

'So are you! Kate, do you miss Angus very much?'

She drew in her breath a little.

'We probably all miss Angus. Father and Keith are working like mad to get their work done. They miss him, too.'

Lachie heard the wobble in her voice, and squeezed her fingers.

'The time will soon pass,' he said comfortingly.

Kate said nothing. It seemed like an eternity before she would ever see Angus again, but she knew Lachie understood.

★ ★ ★

Sally and Caroline were sitting in front of a big fire in the lounge when Kate walked in. Sally's face looked rather white and drawn, and her eyes were shadowed.

She had told Caroline about her headache as soon as she arrived home, but her stepmother had encouraged her to sit down and talk over her worries once again, instead of keeping them bottled up.

'Things are sure to get better soon, Sally,' she said.

'I feel as though I'm in limbo,' Sally said.

'Well, it can't remain like that for ever, and just remember that the family are all behind you.'

Yet in spite of her sympathetic words to Sally, Caroline herself was a little upset.

Gavin had told her proudly of the good work Keith had done in testing a new consignment of wood. He had wanted her to share his pride in Keith, but in doing so, he had to admit that a great deal of hard work was now going to have to be done again.

It was involving the company in more expense, as well as man-hours.

Even now her husband was in the study, poring over plans and cost sheets, and trying to find new ways of working in their present jobs as economically as possible.

Keith had already spent some time on this before Gavin insisted on him going out for the evening.

Young people needed a certain amount of rest and relaxation. The one comfort to Caroline Reid was in knowing that Keith was proving such a help to her husband.

Now she looked up with a smile as Kate came into the room. Since Angus Fraser had left, Caroline Reid had seen the determinedly cheerful look on Kate's face, and how eagerly she ran to collect the mail each morning.

It was easy to guess that Kate's feelings were involved, but her stepmother remained quietly in the background.

If Kate ever wanted to talk to her, then she knew she had a willing and sympathetic ear in her mother.

'Is your headache better?' Kate asked, dropping into a chair beside Sally.

'A bit. Caroline gave me some painkillers. She has a cure for all ills.'

Sally's voice was without the flippancy she sometimes used.

'I'll get you a hot drink, Kate,' Caroline said, rising.

'No need. I'll get it myself,' Kate smiled.

'No, you sit down . . . and talk to Sally.'

Kate turned to look at her sister, seeing her white face and dark-circled eyes. She had been too wrapped up in herself to notice that Sally was worrying again.

They could hear the telephone ringing, and Caroline Reid's voice as she answered it. A moment later she returned to the lounge.

'It's for you, Sally,' she said. 'It . . . it's the hotel, dear.'

Sally went white. Trembling, she rose and went through to lift up the receiver, listening to the deep rich voice of Mr Elliot, the hotel manager. His normal brisk tones had slowed considerably.

'Miss Reid, Sally?' he asked.

'Yes.'

'I . . . er . . . I'm sorry, Sally,' Mr Elliot told her hesitantly. 'I'm afraid I haven't exactly got good news for you.

We have made exhaustive enquiries, but Mrs Naismith's gold brooch just hasn't turned up.'

Sally waited, her heart beginning to beat unevenly.

'I'm afraid we'll have to call in the police after all — reluctant though we are. I think you'd better come back to the hotel.'

Sally was hardly aware that she had mumbled a reply. She was still standing by the phone when her stepmother walked through to find her, and took the receiver out of her icy fingers.

# Out Of The Darkness

In later years. Sally was to remember her journey back to London as the most traumatic experience of her life.

The fact that she was about to be questioned by the police about the loss of a valuable brooch was her idea of a nightmare.

Caroline Reid had been anxious to go with her.

'I don't think you should see this through alone, darling,' Caroline had said, her arms round Sally's slight, rather rigid body.

It was only now she realised how much weight Sally had lost in the past few weeks.

'I think I should be with you.'

'No,' said Sally. 'I don't want you to come.'

As Caroline drew back a little, the young girl turned to her impulsively, and she could see how deeply upset Sally was.

'Please don't misunderstand, Caroline,' she said huskily. 'I'd love you to come, but . . . I feel this is my problem, and I must face it myself.'

'But you need your family to support you. Would you like Kate to go with you?'

'I've had my family to support me, and I don't want Kate either. It's been wonderful of you all, and you'll never know what it has done for me. It has given me the courage to face things on my own. Don't you see?'

Caroline Reid's eyes met her husband's, seeing pride there among all the anxiety.

'I know what you mean, Sally,' he said. 'But if you change your mind in the morning . . . '

He shrugged, not sure how to go on. 'At least phone us as soon as you know anything. Caroline and I will both come to London, if you need us.'

'Thank you, Dad,' Sally said, her

voice trembling. 'I'll let you know what happens.'

There was little sleep for any of them that night, and the following morning Keith drove Sally to the station and saw her on to the London train.

She was quietly dressed in a simple suit, and he thought he had rarely seen his young stepsister looking more attractive.

It was late afternoon by the time Sally arrived back at the hotel, and with part of her mind she was contrasting this arrival with the first day she had walked through the doors of the staff entrance, full of eagerness to take up her new position.

Now, as she greeted one or two friends and colleagues, she felt as though a great barrier had grown up between herself and the rest of the staff. There were welcoming smiles for her, but all eyes were on her nevertheless.

'Mr Elliot would like to see you in his office right away,' Janice Todd, the other young receptionist, told her.

'Thank you, Janice.'

Nervously Sally wiped the palms of her hands with a crumpled handkerchief and knocked on the manager's door.

Would the police be waiting for her, she wondered.

Or would they have to be informed when she arrived. Would she, perhaps, have to go the police station? She had no knowledge of such procedures.

Mrs Naismith was sitting with Mr Elliot when Sally went into the manager's office, and both of them rose to greet her with smiles of welcome.

'Oh, here she is, the poor child,' Mrs Naismith said, coming forward to take her hand. 'I . . . I just don't know what to say to you, Miss Reid.'

'We'd better tell you straightaway that the gold pin has been found.'

Sally felt as though the room was whirling around her, as the tension began to leave her.

'Here . . . sit down, my dear,' Mrs Naismith was saying. 'Oh dear, I blame myself so much. The poor girl must have been through a terrible time. It was all my own fault, my dear. After the ball, I wore the pin on my heavy tweed suit, and somehow it got pushed down between the loose weave of the tweed and the lining.

'It had fallen to the hem of the jacket, and it was only when I felt the prick of the pin through the jacket that I investigated. I should have remembered that I last wore it with the green suit, and examined it all much more carefully . . . '

Sally heard the older woman's voice going on and on, as she went into her explanation, but she was hardly listening to the actual words. She felt sick and faint, realising how little food she had eaten that day.

It was Mr Elliot who turned to the girl, and understood how she was feeling.

'Miss Reid needs something to pick her up . . . Tea and sandwiches for now.' Mr Elliott ordered over the phone and then insisted, when they arrived, that Sally eat every crumb.

'You must be compensated, of course,' Mrs Naismith said. 'We can't expect you to go through such a gruelling time without some sort of reward.'

'Thank you,' Sally said quietly, 'but I want nothing.'

'Oh, but you must have something, my dear.'

'I would just like to settle into my job again,' Sally told Mr Elliot, as she turned to him.

He was smiling, his eyes showing approval and admiration. Sally Reid had grown into a fine girl, in his opinion.

'It's still waiting for you, Sally,' he assured her. 'You can start whenever you feel you want to, though if you'd like a rest . . . '

'I've had a rest, thank you,' Sally said, standing up. 'I'd like to start in the morning, if I may. And I'd like to phone my parents. They were rather worried.'

'By all means. You must phone them straightaway.'

Mr Elliot was thoughtful as Sally excused herself and left the room. The matter wasn't going to be left there, he decided.

Sally didn't fully appreciate that the nightmare was all behind her until she had phoned the family, and listened to their exclamations of relief and delight.

'It's marvellous, darling,' cried Caroline Reid, then passed the phone to her husband, who had rather less to say since underneath he felt angry that Sally had been subjected to it all.

Caroline Reid, however, had made him see that such things were all part of life, and that she knew all along that it would only be a matter of time before Sally was cleared.

Kate and Keith also joined in with good wishes and told her to come back home soon, if she got a free weekend.

'I'll try very hard to put up with you,' Keith told her solemnly.

'Big of you!' Sally laughed, and they

all relaxed. She sounded like her old self again.

Keith looked at the clock as they replaced the phone. He had hoped to go over to Meadowpark, but he and Gavin were working late that evening, and he wondered if Lachie was already over there.

* * *

In fact, Lachie was giving a great deal of thought to his possible date with Moira, and he knew that one way he could gain over Keith was in his knowledge of the countryside which he felt he could share with Moira.

He knew every tree, every plant, wild flower, bird and woodland creature under his care, and he thought that he could do no better than to take Moira for a walk which would let him share his knowledge with her.

Lachie looked smart in his leather jacket, boots and cords, as he rang the bell at Meadowpark. There was no reply, but Lachie could hear Norrie shouting a little tearfully, and Moira's voice raised in reply.

Slowly he pushed open the door, calling out as he went, then suddenly Moira appeared looking slightly flushed.

'Oh, hello, Lachie,' she greeted him. 'Come into the kitchen, please. I could do with your help with Norrie.'

'Why? What's happened?'

'Nothing to get alarmed about, though I'm afraid Alec's got an attack of the jitters. It's Gemma. The baby is on its way and the doctor has just been. He's having Gemma admitted to hospital straightaway.'

'But — but I thought she was staying at home this time . . . '

'Not after Gemma started having trouble with her blood pressure, Lachie. She's better in hospital.'

Gemma was sitting beside the huge kitchen fire looking rather pale but composed. Alec was walking about nervously.

'Don't worry so much,' Gemma told

him. 'It will all be over before you know it.'

'I wish it was!' Alec said fervently.

'Mummy!' cried Norrie, running towards her, and Lachie stepped forward, swinging the small boy into the air and putting him on to his shoulder.

'See what a big chap you are,' he said. 'You don't want to go running to your mummy. You'll have to show her how grown up you are.'

Norman struggled and demanded to be put down, and Lachie set him on his feet.

'You and I are going to do some work for your daddy,' he said. 'I can't do it without you, because I don't know where anything is.'

'I'll show you,' cried Norrie, his troubles forgotten. 'I know where everything is.'

'Great! Where can I start, Alec?'

'What? Oh, you're all dressed up . . . '

'I can borrow some overalls from you.'

'Well, Frank Lawson is coping OK, but ... ' Alec outlined one or two remaining jobs, gratitude in his voice, though he turned to Norrie.

'You should be in bed, young man!'

'Let him help Lachie, then I'll put him to bed,' Moira said and her smile when she looked at Lachie warmed his heart.

Later, when Alec returned from the hospital, Lachie volunteered to go down to Hazelbank and tell the family.

'I was going to ring them,' Moira said worriedly, 'but it's difficult to explain things properly over the phone.'

'Mrs Reid would understand,' Lachie answered her. 'She was a nurse, you know, and Kate is very level-headed.'

He was looking at Moira when he spoke about Kate, and he smiled as their eyes met. Perhaps Moira would understand that he now recognised Kate as a good friend, and nothing more.

'I'd better go, then,' Lachie said, 'but I'll come up again tomorrow, Moira, in case there's anything I can do.'

'Thanks, Lachie,' she said sincerely.

Mr Reid and Keith were still working late when Lachie called at Hazelbank, but Caroline Reid smiled her welcome, and invited Lachie into the lounge.

'I can't stay,' he apologised. 'I've only called to say that Gemma has gone to hospital. The baby is due soon now . . . '

'Oh, Lachie!' Kate cried, her eyes bright. 'I'll phone straightaway.'

'She only just gone in,' Lachie said.

'I know, but just in case . . . '

She dashed away into the hall, and they could hear her excited voice, then the receiver being replaced.

'No news yet,' she told them, coming back into the room.

Lachie rose to say good night.

'If I can do anything to help, you've only got to phone,' he told both women. 'I've got plenty to do at work, but maybe I can manage to find a spare moment more easily then Keith or Mr Reid. Don't be afraid to ask.'

'Thank you, Lachie.' Caroline Reid said gently, and Kate nodded and smiled.

'If you want to go on up to bed, Kate,' said Caroline, after Lachie had gone, 'I'll sit up for your father and Keith.'

'No, I wouldn't sleep. We'll wait for them together. They'll probably be tired when they get home.'

\* \* \*

But Gavin Reid and Keith were far from tired as they looked proudly on the last stages of their labours at West Lodge, with Bob Simpson standing beside them.

'It's been a big job,' said Mr Reid, 'but I can't remember one more satisfying. We can all take the credit for it, too; you for that fine wood you found us, Keith, and you, Bob, for that panelling. I don't know why you fought shy of it in the first place.'

Bob's eyes glowed with pride.

'I never really thought I could do it.' Bob Simpson admitted. 'I hesitated when I thought of the time involved, and how easily I might ruin it. It might have meant the loss of precious time and materials. But, with Angus away, I had to take the plunge and now I'm very grateful for the chance.'

'I'm grateful that you took it, Bob,' said Mr Reid. 'It means that I needn't worry about taking on another job like this, if you are able to help.'

'Just a few loose ends to tie up, and the job is finished,' Keith said, as he leafed over a few papers. 'Mr Richmond is coming up to West Lodge next week. It should all be ready for him to step into.'

Gavin Reid gave a small sigh of satisfaction as they said good night to Bob Simpson.

'The great thing is that we're pulling a bit straighter, Keith,' he said to his stepson, as they walked home together.

'I think it might be a nice idea if we all go out for a meal to celebrate one evening soon. Suppose we book a table at the hotel?'

'That would be marvellous,' said Keith with enthusiasm.

'I'll ask Caroline as soon as we go in,' said Gavin Reid, as he opened the door.

Caroline Reid heard the key in the lock and she hurried out into the hall with Kate close behind her.

'Hello, darling!' Gavin called. 'Sorry we're so late, but we've got good news for you. West Lodge is almost finished.'

'That's marvellous,' his wife said absently, and Gavin Reid turned quickly to look at her.

'What's happened?' he asked.

'Nothing to worry about,' she assured him. 'It's Gemma. She's gone into hospital, and her baby should be born soon.'

'Oh!'

Gavin's eyes lit up. 'I'd call that good news,' he said. 'How is Gemma? Have you been in touch with the hospital?'

'Yes, but there's no news for us yet.

Her . . . her blood pressure is a little high.'

'We had planned to book a table at the hotel for the four of us to have a celebration dinner.' Gavin Reid turned to his stepson. 'We'd better postpone it for a while, Keith. We could have more to celebrate than completing West Lodge.'

'Quite right.' Caroline smiled. 'And I suspect you're both very tired, so I suggest bed for us all as soon as we've had supper. OK?'

'OK,' Kate agreed. 'I think I'll go up now.'

But Kate lay sleepless for a long time, thinking about her sister. She remembered that Gemma had been ill early in her pregnancy, and how upset and worried they had been.

Would that have an effect on Gemma now? And what about her baby?

Kate decided that the following day she would walk over to Meadowpark to see how well Moira was coping. It would help if she had something to do and time would hang heavily otherwise, as it was her day off.

Kate's thoughts turned to Sally. Should she ring her about Gemma? She decided to wait for some proper news.

As she planned her day, Kate's thoughts once again turned to Angus as she wondered how he was getting on, so far away. Slowly her eyelids drooped, and she slept.

★ ★ ★

The following morning there was an air of tension in the house as Caroline Reid shook her head, having once again telephoned the hospital. There was still no news.

'I'll go over to Meadowpark,' Kate said, as she poured herself a cup of coffee. 'Moira may need some help.'

'Why not bring Norrie here?' Caroline offered. 'What do you think, darling?'

Gavin nodded. 'If it wouldn't upset him,' he agreed, 'and if you think you can cope, Caroline.'

'I'll have Kate to help settle him in, and I'm well used to small boys,' she said, smiling at her son.

He stood up, towering above her, tall and thin.

'I'm certainly a small boy,' he agreed, while they all laughed. 'Oh, there's the post.'

'I'll get it,' Kate said, and ran towards the front door. Her heart leapt when she saw an air-mail letter in Angus's familiar handwriting. She slipped it into her pocket, going back to the kitchen to share out the post to the other members of the family.

Later, in her bedroom, she read Angus's letter. It was closely written, and mainly described the fascinating country in which he was becoming so deeply involved. This time he did mention Felicity Powers.

*There is such a wonderful detail on all the wildlife, he wrote, and colours that are almost impossible to create in paint. Felicity Powers, the chairman's* daughter, is taking some terrific photographs though.

I learned a little about photography at art college, but I realised when I saw how professionally she went about her job, how little I really knew.

I find it all fascinating, though, Kate, and I'll always be grateful for this opportunity. There's just something about the place that inspires you to do your best . . .

Kate read to the end of the letter, realising that Angus was completely wrapped up in his commission. She should be pleased for him. She should be glad that everything was going well.

But, somehow, Angus seemed further away than ever. She tried to find even a small hint of a personal note in the letter, but it was the type of letter which could have been written by anyone.

Slowly she zipped up her anorak and put on her walking shoes. She would walk over to Meadowpark, and perhaps the fresh air would clear away a few cobwebs.

At Meadowpark, Kate was aware of the anxiety and tension straightaway, and Norrie was also sensing the strain and proving to be as difficult as possible.

Kate saw, however, that Moira was becoming an expert at coping with him.

'Alec is as much of a liability as Norrie.' She smiled to Kate. 'Talk about pacing the floor! Thank goodness he's still got Frank Lawson to help him. Lachie is coming over, too.'

'They'll give him moral support,' Kate said, smiling a little.

'Right,' Moira agreed.

'Norrie, if you don't drink that milk and eat your biscuit, you'll need to go hungry!'

'Would it help if I took him to Hazelbank?' asked Kate.

'Would it! I'd get through here in half the time, and I'd be able to get Gemma's room ready for her.'

'Say no more!' Kate said, and turned

to her young nephew. 'Do you know where to find your holiday case?'

Norrie stared at her a little sulkily, then he cheered up at the prospect of going away.

'It's in the cupboard upstairs, Auntie Kate. Am I going on holiday? Am I going to the seaside, and are Mummy and Daddy coming?'

'Not until your summer holiday!' Kate laughed. 'I just want you to come to Hazelbank and stay with Granny and Grandad, and Uncle Keith and me.'

Norrie's face fell again.

'I want Mummy,' he whispered, his voice trembling.

'Well, Mum is still very busy in the hospital, but she'll be home soon with your new baby. Aunt Moira has lots to do getting the house ready for Mummy and the baby. We'll go to Hazelbank, then you can come back, after Mummy gets home.'

'Along with the baby?' Norrie asked. He had been hearing about his expected brother or sister for some time.

'Yes.'

'I don't think I want it now,' he added, and the two girls sighed as they stared at one another.

'Come on and we'll pack that case,' Kate said, 'and you can choose two toys to take with you. Which two do you want? What are your favourites?'

Rather listlessly, Norrie chose his teddy and a small tractor. Without giving him too long to think about it, Kate shepherded him towards the door.

'I'll drive you home,' Moira offered. She had recently passed her test.

'Thanks, Moira. We'll get this young man home before he's had time to change his mind.'

It was Keith who helped to settle the small boy. He had bought a simple set of dominoes, using pretty pictures and the two of them began to play.

The phone rang and Kate was still smiling when she went to answer it. A moment later her heart began to beat with excitement, as she recognised Alec's voice.

'I'm at the hospital, Kate,' he said. 'It's a little girl.'

'A girl!' cried Kate. 'Oh, Alec, how lovely! I must tell the family straight-away.'

Putting down the receiver, she rushed through to the lounge.

'It's a girl,' she said breathlessly. 'Isn't that marvellous.'

'Oh, thank goodness,' Gavin Reid said.

'Are they both well?' his wife asked.

'I think so, though I forgot to ask,' said Kate. 'Alec was so excited.'

'Then you don't know the baby's weight?'

'Never mind all the details,' Gavin interrupted. 'Just as long as it's all over.'

Norman was staring up at them, and he suddenly threw down his dominoes.

'I don't want a girl,' he said. 'I want a boy to play with.'

'You'd better practise these domi-noes,' Keith said easily. 'She's still just a baby, but you don't want her to beat you some day, do you?'

Slowly Norrie took the dominoes up again, even as his grandfather proposed that they had a drink to celebrate.

It was Caroline Reid who still sat in her chair rather uneasily, and that evening after they had put Norrie to bed, she slipped down and telephoned the hospital.

She was unaware of her husband standing behind her as she began to ask for details about Gemma. She quickly realised that her stepdaughter's health was still giving some cause for concern.

Slowly she put down the telephone. Somehow she would have to keep it from her husband that Gemma was not out of the woods.

'Well?' he asked behind her. 'How is Gemma and the baby? Did you get all your questions answered?'

'Oh. Gavin! You startled me,' she cried, then bit her lip, wondering what to say.

# Anxious Days

Gavin Reid's face paled as he saw the anxiety in his wife's eyes.

'What's wrong?' he asked sharply. 'Has anything happened to Gemma?'

She paused for a moment, tempted to speak to him reassuringly, but almost immediately she changed her mind. It was better for her to explain a little since Gavin would probably worry less if he knew all the facts.

'It's Gemma's blood pressure. It just hasn't gone down after the baby was born. She will still have to rest, darling, and she will need careful nursing, though everything possible will be done for her in hospital . . . '

She went into a few technical details so that Gavin would understand exactly what was happening. However, he still looked worried and she began to grow alarmed when she saw the lack of colour in his face.

The past few months had been a great strain for Gavin, she thought, as she remembered his efforts at trying to pull the firm on to an even keel.

She had also been aware of his deep anxiety about Sally, and the restless nights he had spent until they heard that there was no further need for worry.

And now it was Gemma's turn, thought Caroline Reid unhappily. There was a strong bond between her husband and his eldest daughter, and she knew he wouldn't have a minute's peace until Gemma was well on the way to recovery.

'I think you should go to bed and rest,' Caroline Reid told her husband firmly. 'It won't help Gemma if — if you get a bit run down again.'

'I have a few things to see to,' he said rather wearily.

'Nothing that Keith can't handle, I'm sure.'

'What is it that Keith can't handle?'

Keith asked with a grin, as his mother and stepfather walked into the lounge. His smile faded as he saw the warning look in his mother's eyes.

'If you mean those two cottages in Tordale that are going to be converted into one house,' he went on, 'I can see the architect for you. We worked together once before when Newbank House was turned into a hotel.'

Gavin Reid nodded. He didn't feel energetic enough to discuss business with Keith, and allowed himself to be persuaded to have an early night. It was a long time since he felt so tired.

The following day Keith found himself with more work and responsibility than he'd ever had in his life, but the decisions he had to make were coming more and more easily. It seemed a long time ago, he thought with a sigh of thankfulness, that he'd had to go to London and see Angus because things were getting on top of him.

Now he seemed to take it all in his

stride, knowing who could best tackle any particular job, and also knowing that his costing would be fair and accurate.

That evening as he went over the work with his stepfather, Keith felt a deep inner sense of satisfaction. So often he had listened to Gavin Reid and Angus thrashing out problems while he stood by as an onlooker, but now Gavin was turning to him as he had once depended on Angus.

'This all seems to be very good, Keith,' Gavin said.

'We still can't afford to let up, though,' Keith said, as he leafed over the work sheets. 'There isn't a great deal of profit in a lot of this work.'

'No, you're right there,' his stepfather agreed.

'Anyway, not to worry,' Keith said confidently. 'I'll soon get more business in. I'm beginning to make a few contacts.'

Gavin Reid nodded. For the time being he was glad to leave everything in his stepson's capable hands. He'd had a word on the telephone with Alec, who assured him Keith was coping very well.

Gavin Reid had always had a liking and respect for his son-in-law, but never more so than now when the worry of Gemma lay between them.

'I wish there was more I could do to help you, Alec,' he told him.

'Lachie Fraser is coming over this evening,' Alec said. 'Then I'll go in and sit with Gemma again. I'm sure everything will be all right, if we are patient.'

'I'll be in to see her as soon as I can,' his father-in-law assured him.

★ ★ ★

Moira Johnstone was on her own, coping with Norrie, who had insisted on going back home to his father, when Lachie walked over to Meadowpark that evening.

'I'm going to help you, Uncle

Lachie,' Norrie said, pushing his feet into a tiny pair of blue gumboots. 'I can show you where everything is.'

Lachie sighed, knowing that everything would now take twice as long, but he realised the small boy needed humouring as much as anyone.

'I don't think you should bother Uncle Lachie, Norrie,' Moira began.

'No, don't stop him,' Lachie said. 'Let him help until he's tired.'

He saw the smile of gratitude in her eyes and his heart bounded. He could no longer deny to himself how much he loved Moira Johnstone.

Even if she hadn't been at Meadowpark he would be glad to come up each evening and help Alec out, but she turned the work into tasks of joy and pleasure, just by coming to watch and talking to him while he worked.

The young calves had to be fed and a great deal of cleaning up had to be done, though Frank Lawson had already coped with most of it. The work was soon done.

Norrie had his arms outstretched, herding the geese while Lachie locked them in, then he turned to walk back to the house with Moira. The evening had grown quiet and still, and he felt there was no need for words between them.

But Moira grew matter-of-fact, and cheerfully talkative after they had both put Norrie to bed and set about tidying up his toy box. The police car which he had insisted on taking to bed had been located at the bottom of the box.

'What's the new baby's name?' Lachie asked. 'Has that been decided yet?'

'I think everyone has been too anxious about Gemma,' Moira answered. 'Though I rather think she fancies Alison. It was her mother's middle name.'

'I like Alison,' Lachie said, 'though . . . though for my money, there's nothing to beat Moira for a name.'

Moira had turned away, though he could see the warm colour in her cheeks, she was busy picking up Norrie's discarded boots.

'Just look at the state of these,' she said, 'all scuffed. I'll have to clean them.'

'Never mind the boots for now, Moira,' Lachie said, suddenly determined not to be put off.

Each day that passed was showing him more and more clearly how he felt about her, and he knew there could be no other girl for him.

For years he had thought it was Kate he loved, but now he realised it was Moira who was all he ever wanted.

She turned to look at him uncertainly.

'Lachie, I . . . '

'No, don't say anything until you hear me out,' he told her. 'You must know how much I love you now, Moira. There's just nobody else for me but you, and I won't ever be happy unless you feel the same way — enough to marry me, Moira. Will you? Will you marry me?'

He was putting it badly, thought Lachie, as he felt the reserve still in her.

Moira had turned away and was aimlessly holding a small T-shirt in her hands. Lachie took it from her, and pulled her into his arms, determined to assure her that he meant every word he said.

'Say you'll marry me, Moira,' he pleaded.

Her eyes were wide as she stared at him. For a long time she had taught herself to accept the fact that it was Kate whom Lachie loved.

She had watched Lachie's eyes as they followed Kate and Angus, and she had fought down her own feelings.

It seemed to her that Lachie had only turned to her after seeing that Kate would always love Angus, and she had no wish to be second best.

Moira had seen how you had to work at a marriage even when there was true love between the partners, as there was between Alec and Gemma, and she knew she must be very sure of Lachie before she accepted.

Lachie felt upset as she didn't reply.

'Is it Keith Drummond?' he was asking, even as her thoughts darted this way and that.

'What?' Moira looked at Lachie's puzzled face.

'Has Keith asked you to marry him?' Lachie persisted.

'No,' Moira assured him. 'It's not Keith.'

'Well?'

'I — I'm not sure how to explain this, Lachie. You've taken me by surprise. Are you sure this is what you want? I mean, what about Kate?'

'She means nothing to me, Moira. I realised that a long time ago. You're the only one I could love now. Please say you'll marry me.'

But Moira shook her head. 'I can't give you an answer yet. Please, let me think about it.'

Lachie looked downcast.

'I need to be sure, Lachie,' she went on. 'Not only of my feelings, but of yours. I hardly know you. If I were to say yes now, we'd be rushing into things. Perhaps in a few months' time you'd regret this — realise it was only because Kate had rejected you that . . . '

'No!' Lachie almost shouted. 'I'm over all that. I love you, Moira, not Kate.'

'But we need to be sure. Please, give me some time.'

Before Lachie could say any more, the door banged and they heard Alec's footsteps.

'Hello, you two,' he greeted them. 'Did you manage to get Norrie up to bed?'

Moira looked flushed.

'How — how is Gemma?' she asked.

'She seems to be sleeping a lot,' Alec said. 'They say she is comfortable. But her blood pressure still isn't back to normal.'

Lachie bit his lip. He felt rather frustrated and disappointed that he had been unable to convince Moira of his feelings.

'I'm sorry, Alec,' he said sincerely. 'How is the baby?'

'Fine. She's very tiny, just over five pounds, but they say she'll grow all the quicker. She's fair, like Gemma,' he told them, and Lachie put his hand on his friend's arm in sympathy.

'Everything's been taken care of here,' he said, 'and I'll try to get over earlier tomorrow evening. If you want me before then, just give me a ring.'

Alec nodded.

'I — I'd better be off,' said Lachie, and Moira walked with him to the door.

'At least you'll think about my proposal,' he insisted, and she nodded to him soberly.

'I'll think about it, Lachie,' she agreed. 'Good night.' With that, Lachie had to be content.

\* \* \*

The following day, Keith answered the phone rather absently as he leafed over some correspondence, though his eyes sharpened when he heard the deep voice at the other end.

'I would like to speak to Mr Reid, please. This is Mr Richmond of West Lodge.'

'Mr Reid isn't in today,' Keith said. 'Is there anything I can do? I'm Keith Drummond, his stepson.'

'Ah, yes, Mr Drummond . . . ' The deep voice tailed off a little. 'Will Mr Reid be free on Saturday, if I call in to see him at Hazelbank? It would be some time in the afternoon.'

Keith paused. 'I think that would be all right. Mr Richmond, though I'll have to check with Mr Reid.'

'If it is inconvenient, then perhaps he'll give me a ring,' his caller continued. 'I'll be at West Lodge for the next month.'

'Very well, Mr Richmond.'

Keith put down the phone, biting his lip. Just why did Mr Richmond want to see his stepfather? Surely there could be nothing wrong in the work that had been done?

The time seemed to drag before he

returned home after the workshop had closed for the night, and Keith lost no time in hurrying into the sitting-room, where his stepfather had been resting.

'Mr Richmond has been on the phone,' Keith said. 'He wants to call in to see you on Saturday afternoon. Can you let him know if it's all right?'

'What? Who? Mr Richmond?' Gavin Reid said, laying aside his magazine. 'Did he say what he wanted?'

'No. Just to see you.'

'Well, didn't you tell him that he's not at all well?' Caroline asked. 'I don't think you ought to be worried with business matters, darling. Why don't you ring and put it off for a week.'

'Of course I'll see Mr Richmond,' Gavin Reid said in a sharper tone than he normally used with his wife. 'I'm as anxious as Keith to know why he wants to see me.'

'But, Gavin . . . '

'Don't fuss, Caroline,' he said. 'I'm perfectly all right, and Keith will ring and confirm the appointment, won't you, Keith?'

Slowly Keith nodded, seeing the tinge of colour in his stepfather's cheeks. Caroline Reid turned away, though her eyes still showed their concern. Her husband only felt better because he had been resting, but she could see how quickly he tired, and sometimes his colour was poor.

Caroline Reid went off to prepare the evening meal, but as she worked in the kitchen, her eyes were sober. Looking after her husband was going to mean even more careful thought, she told herself, if she was going to shield him from overstrain.

It was no use being straightforward or he would think she was fussing. She would have to shelter him without ever letting him see that this was so.

In the meantime, Mr Richmond would be very welcome, since he was calling to see her husband in his own home. She would see that the visit was as relaxing as possible.

'Hello, Caroline,' Kate called, coming to poke her head round the kitchen door. 'Anything I can do?'

'Work yourself up an appetite, dear,' was the reply. 'You've been picking away like a wee bird recently. I'm going to the hospital to see Gemma right after tea. Are you coming with me?'

'Sure thing,' Kate said. 'I'll be glad to see her looking more like her old self, though. Maybe we can get a glimpse of the baby, too. Do you know if they've settled on the name Alison?'

'We can ask Gemma tonight. It's one of my favourite names, and it seems to suit the baby, somehow. I've asked Mrs Simpson to do the washing-up for us, since Keith is going out.'

Kate's eyes met Caroline's, knowing they understood one another. Until her father was once again on top form, Caroline Reid wasn't leaving him on his own.

Gemma seemed a little better that evening, though Kate could see how her stepmother still insisted on her resting quietly, and only having two visitors at a time.

Kate was very quiet on the way home, and Mrs Simpson was already getting into her coat when they arrived back at Hazelbank.

'Sally has been on the telephone,' she informed them. 'She says she'll come straight home.'

'Why?' asked Kate.

'To see Gemma, of course.' Mrs Simpson looked surprised. 'I had to tell her poor Gemma was still not well with her blood pressure. She didn't seem to know.'

'She didn't know because we didn't tell her,' said Kate, obviously annoyed. 'There seemed to be no reason to drag Sally all the way home so soon after making the long journey back to London, unless it was absolutely necessary. Gemma isn't well, and we're concerned for her, but it isn't an emergency, Mrs Simpson.'

Mrs Simpson's pleasant face flushed. It was rare for Kate to turn on her.

'Well . . . I, I'm sorry, I'm sure,' she began.

'You weren't to know, Mrs Simpson,' Caroline Reid said, smoothing it over. 'Thank you for holding the fort for us.'

Her eyes pleaded for the older woman's understanding, and Mrs Simpson turned away, somewhat mollified. Kate must be under a strain with her sister so ill. It wasn't like her to be out of sorts.

Caroline Reid was thinking the same thing as she looked at her stepdaughter. Kate looked pale and tired, and when she thought about it, there had not been many letters from Angus Fraser recently.

Perhaps that accounted for some of her edginess. She would like to have asked Kate what was troubling her, but this time she felt instinctively it was something Kate had to sort out on her own.

★   ★   ★

On Saturday morning Caroline Reid rose early, determined that everything would be as comfortable as possible for Mr Richmond's visit.

It wasn't easy to polish and tidy up the sitting-room while Gavin occupied it, since he seemed to require a great many books and magazines to keep him happy.

At least today he wouldn't need to lie down. The enforced rest was beginning to pay off.

Glancing at her watch, she went to the phone to ring the hospital, and after a conversation with the sister in charge of Gemma's ward, she put down the receiver, breathing a small prayer of thankfulness. Gemma's blood pressure had dropped, and she was now on the way to recovery.

Quickly she made a pot of tea, and carried a tray up to the bedroom, where Gavin Reid was already awake, pulling back the curtains to allow the sunshine to stream in.

'I've just phoned the hospital, darling,' she said.

'And?'

He stared at her intently.

'Gemma's blood pressure is down. It won't be long now until she's fully recovered.'

'Well, thank goodness for that!' he said fervently. 'Will she really be OK, Caroline?'

'Home next week or so the doctor hopes.'

They stared at one another for a long moment, and Caroline knew they didn't need to put their feelings into words.

Together they were sharing the ups and downs of life.

'You'd better get up soon,' she told him, laughingly. 'You've got Mr Richmond coming to see you today, don't forget.'

'I'm not likely to,' Gavin said. 'I hope you're going to cook me an enormous breakfast. I'm starving.'

'I might just do that. Oh, there's the post!'

A quick glance through the mail showed her that there was still no letter for Kate from Angus Fraser, and Caroline Reid's eyes darkened with disappointment. She was beginning to worry a little about Kate.

In the afternoon Mr Richmond arrived in good time, smiling with pleasure when Caroline showed him into the sitting-room. Gavin Reid had risen to greet him, holding out his hand for a warm handshake.

'I hope I'm not interrupting anything, Mr Reid,' said Mr Richmond, as he sat down comfortably by the fireside, 'but I'm sure that when we've had a chat, you'll excuse me for coming to see you like this.'

'I'm delighted to see you. Mr Richmond. I hope everything is OK at West Lodge.'

'Everything is beautiful. In fact, that's really why I'm here. I've just learned that Tordale Castle may be coming up for renovation.'

'Tordale Castle!'

'Yes. I expect you know it has been closed to the public for the past few months, but there are plans afoot to turn it into a museum and art gallery.

'It's a thriving town now, and should have some building of this kind. Very soon all this will be put forward at a meeting, and tenders invited, so I thought I would bring it to your notice.

'I have no influence as such, Mr Reid, you understand, but I am keen on preserving places of historic interest. I can think of no-one more able to tackle the renovation of Tordale Castle than yourself.

'It would give me great pleasure if you landed this contract, and if you wish to use my name in any way, please feel free to do so.'

Mr Reid sat back, his eyes bright at the thought. He had been round Tordale Castle a few years ago when it was open to the public, and he remembered his interest in the place at that time.

Even then there were parts of it he would have loved to have renovated, and he knew it would be a job after his own heart.

It would be a big contract, too, and if he landed it, he knew his firm would be in the clear financially, though it would all have to be costed carefully.

At the same time, he knew the practical experience they had gained in solving the problems at West Lodge would be invaluable.

'I'm very grateful you've brought this to my notice, Mr Richmond,' he said, eagerly. 'I'll certainly tender for the contract. I'm sure it will be more than helpful that you're prepared to recommend my firm.'

'I think West Lodge, itself, is splendid recommendation,' said Mr Richmond warmly. 'I shall be very disappointed indeed if you don't get it. Though, somehow, I don't think you'll have too much competition.'

Gavin Reid smiled, though he knew he would not count his chickens.

There was a light tap at the door, and Caroline Reid came in, pushing a laden trolley. Mr Richmond rose to help her.

'I hope you aren't going to say you haven't time for tea, Mr Richmond,' she said, smiling.

'No indeed!' he assured her. 'Wild horses wouldn't drag me away after a sight of such a lovely tea. Thank you very much.'

★　★　★

It was a happy afternoon, though Caroline could see that her husband was excited by something, and he could hardly wait to tell the family after Mr Richmond had gone.

'If we landed the contract, everything would be fine again,' he said, with enthusiasm. 'I know we could do it, now that you are doing so well, Keith, and with Angus back . . . '

'I wouldn't count on Angus coming back,' said Kate, quickly.

'No, of course not. I'd rather forgotten that he is now a well-known artist,' said her father. 'But even without Angus, we could do it. Some of the men were just getting into their stride at West Lodge. It would be a contract we could get our teeth into.'

'I hope you get it, Dad,' Kate said gently, though her stepmother thought she could see a glint of tears in her eyes.

Kate never allowed any unhappy feeling to cloud things for other people, but Caroline fervently hoped she wasn't going to be hurt by Angus Fraser. She longed to take the girl in her arms, but Kate's nature was quite different from Sally's. She knew instinctively she couldn't comfort her in the way she had her younger sister.

The bell shrilled, jerking Caroline out of her thoughts, and Keith rose to his feet. He, too, was trying to keep his excitement under control.

'I'll get it!' he said.

A moment later Sally was being ushered into the sitting-room.

'Look who's here!' Keith said behind her. 'It's . . . '

' . . . the bad penny.' Sally finished, slanting a smile at him, though there was an anxious expression on her face.

'Oh, Sally. I was so annoyed with Mrs Simpson for worrying you,' said Kate, coming forward to kiss her sister. 'You must have had such a journey.'

'That's all right.' Sally said. 'I don't like being kept in the dark. I had to know about Gemma, and I do so want to see the baby.'

'Gemma is better, darling,' Caroline Reid assured her. 'You'll be able to see both of them tomorrow, and I expect they'll be home next week. I rather think I'll have to see what can be done about nursing her at Meadowpark for another week or two . . . '

'Well, thank goodness for that,' Sally said fervently. 'I say, you have had a spread. I'll just help myself, if I may.'

Kate went to get another cup, while Sally piled her plate up with sandwiches from the trolley.

'I feel like celebrating,' she said

happily. 'As a matter of fact, I was coming home this weekend anyway, because I've got something very special to tell you all.'

# Waiting Her Answer

Sally laughed when she saw the startled expressions on the faces of each member of the family.

'What sort of news?' her father was asking.

'Oh. I haven't gone off and married someone behind your back,' she assured him, her eyes twinkling. 'No, I'm going to Switzerland! I've been offered a complete course on Hotel Management. Mr Elliot has arranged it for me. Mrs Naismith has offered to help with the finance, and this time I've decided to accept her offer.

'I'm really interested in making hotel work my career, and Mr Elliot feels I'll do very well in it. Isn't it exciting?'

Kate had never seen her young sister looking so happy. She could hardly believe that Sally was the same girl who had been so restless and bored at home.

Now she was so much more contented and mature.

Caroline Reid stepped forward to kiss her stepdaughter.

'I'm very happy for you, darling,' she said, and Gavin Reid also gave his daughter a warm hug as he congratulated her. However, his eyes were more grave. He was going to miss Sally.

Kate was rather quiet as the family discussed Sally's plans with a great deal of excitement and laughter. Excusing herself, she went into the garden for some fresh air.

She was standing, deep in thought, when Sally came out a few minutes later. Sally stood by her, saying nothing. She realised something was wrong.

In the past it had always been she who had gone to Kate for help and comfort and now Sally realised it was her turn.

Finally she spoke.

'Is everything OK. Kate?'

'Everything is fine. What could be wrong?' Kate asked evasively.

'Oh, I . . . I don't know. I just felt there was something. I wondered if it was because I am going away on the course. I mean, you don't really mind, do you, Kate? I know it rather leaves you on your own.'

'Oh, darling, of course I don't mind,' Kate cried, turning to reassure Sally. 'I'm on my own when you're in London, you know.'

'Yes, but . . . '

The younger girl caught a glint of tears in Kate's eyes, and suddenly she realised what might be upsetting Kate.

'How is Angus?' she asked bluntly.

'Oh . . . fine . . . I think. I . . . I haven't heard from him for a week or two. He's probably busy.'

'Of course he'll be busy.' Sally agreed, turning to go.

She knew now what was making her sister unhappy, but she also knew she could do nothing to put it right.

'Good night, Kate,' she said softly.

''Night,' Kate said, 'and don't worry about me, Sally. I'm just very happy that things are going so well for you.'

The following morning Caroline Reid was putting down the phone when Sally came in for breakfast.

'It looks as though you needn't go any farther than Meadowpark to see Gemma,' she said brightly. 'She and the baby are going home today.'

'That's marvellous,' Sally said, and the rest of the family were equally pleased when they all assembled for breakfast.

'It will mean a lot of work for Moira, though,' Kate said thoughtfully.

'Yes, I've been thinking about that,' her stepmother answered. 'In fact, I think I ought to stay at Meadowpark for the next week, and just keep an eye on Gemma and the baby. What do you say, darling?'

She turned to Gavin, who grinned at her.

'So it's Gemma's turn to be cosseted!' he teased.

'Yes, but I'll go only if you promise to behave,' she told him. 'No overdoing it when my back is turned.'

'Don't worry, I've learned my lesson,' he assured her. 'I think it's a good idea for you to stay with Gemma for the next week. She and Alec will be very grateful, darling, and so will I.'

'I'll ring Moira, then, and see if she has no objections.'

\*　\*　\*

Moira Johnstone breathed a sigh of relief when Mrs Reid offered to come and stay at Meadowpark.

The past few weeks had been quite a strain on her, and at the back of her mind was the thought that Lachie was waiting for an answer to his proposal. She had lain awake at nights, wondering what that answer should be.

She was always aware of Lachie living nearby, occasionally catching sight of him as he tramped across the fields.

She needed to get away to think things out. Sometimes she wanted to rush to the phone and tell him that she would marry him whenever he wanted, then caution would creep in. Marriage was so final, and she had to be very sure.

'Would you need me to be here, Mrs Reid?' she asked Caroline, after they had discussed the matter fully.

Caroline Reid's quick ear could detect the strain in the young girl's voice. Moira was really very young to have had so much responsibility over the past few weeks.

On the other hand, she didn't want Moira to feel that she was being pushed out.

'Well, of course it would be very nice to have your help, dear,' she said warmly, 'but I wonder if it wouldn't be a good idea if you had a short holiday from Meadowpark even for just a few days. You could do with a break.'

'It would be nice to go home for a little while,' Moira agreed.

'Then you must do just that,' Caroline Reid told her. 'I'll come over to Meadowpark tomorrow morning, and take over. Tell Gemma not to worry about a thing.'

She put down the phone thoughtfully. She liked Moira very much, and at one time she had wondered if she and Keith might fall in love. However, their friendship hadn't blossomed that far.

Keith was still wrapped up in his career. Perhaps that was just as well, she thought, as she went to find her husband. She was proud that he and her son had drawn so close together.

The following evening Kate helped Sally to pack up the personal possessions she wanted to take to Switzerland.

During the afternoon Sally had walked over to Meadowpark to see Gemma and the new baby.

Gemma still looked very pale and tired, but there was a new happiness and contentment about her, as she proudly showed off baby Alison.

'Oh, Gemma, she's really sweet,' Sally said, awed by the neatness and delicacy of the new baby as she bent over the carry-cot. 'Just look at those tiny fingers.'

'Yes, she is lovely, though I say it myself,' Gemma agreed.

Norrie came bounding into the bedroom where his mother had to rest each afternoon.

'That's our baby, Aunt Sally,' he reminded her. 'I don't think you'd better take her away. You don't know all about babies like my mummy and granny.'

Sally was about to give him a sharp reminder to remember his manners, but she could see the touch of anxiety in the small boy. He was full of the pride of possession, and the relief of having his mother home again.

'Of course she's your baby,' she agreed. 'And no-one will take her away. She belongs to your mummy and daddy — and you!'

'She can have my new tractor,' said Norrie generously.

'Kate will be over tomorrow,' said Sally, turning to her sister, 'on her halfday. She . . . ' Sally hesitated, then decided to say nothing about her fears for Kate.

Gemma had enough worry about, trying to regain her own health and strength. 'She'll be thrilled to see the baby, too,' she finished.

'It's lovely having visitors,' Gemma said. 'I feel very pampered. Kate managed to come to the hospital, but it's much nicer at home.'

'I'll write to you often from Switzerland,' Sally promised.

'It seems odd to think you are going abroad. Isn't it strange what twists and turns life has in store for us? I would have thought you would be the one to marry young.'

Sally shrugged. 'I don't know why you should think that.'

'I wondered about David Martin at one time — that young hotel manager.'

'He is a good friend, nothing more.' Sally smiled. 'No, I'm happy to be 'Aunt Sally' for a while yet, Gemma. I love my independence.'

Gemma nodded. She drew her small son closer to her, and glanced at the sleeping baby in the small pink carry-cot.

Now that her health and strength were coming back, she felt her own life was very full, and she didn't envy her young sister.

'Just be happy,' she told Sally gently.

Sally nodded. She had a lump in her throat as she kissed her sister and her family goodbye. It might be quite a while before she saw them all again.

'Don't forget to keep me posted about Gemma and the baby, and anything else of interest,' Sally told Kate that evening, as they sorted out her possessions.

'I won't!' Kate said. 'What a mess you've got your stuff into! You'll have to be tidier than this in Switzerland.'

'I am tidier now. I had to be in the flat, or my stuff would have become mixed up with June's and Marion's.'

'Well, at least you're acquiring some dress sense now,' Kate assured her. 'You look very smart these days.'

'Thank you, ma'am,' said Sally, bowing, though her pink cheeks showed she was pleased with the compliment.

She looked rather critically at Kate. Her sister could also do with a holiday, she decided, but somehow Kate had always been so good at managing her own affairs, that Sally had never given or tried to give her advice.

'Just remember to write often,' she repeated finally. 'It's exciting to go away, but I'll want to know about home.'

'Of course I will,' Kate said. 'Though if I know you, I'll have to write two letters to every scrappy one I'll get from you. We'll want to hear your news, too.'

'I'll remember,' Sally promised.

★   ★   ★

However, after her sister had gone the following morning, Kate began to realise just how lonely she would be.

It had been a quiet morning in the

post office, and the house was empty when she returned home at lunch-time.

Mrs Simpson had left a note to say that there was a casserole in the oven, and a freshly-made apple pie. Her father and Keith had already eaten their lunch, and were now very busy working on the tender for Tordale Castle.

Sometimes, in the midst of the hustle and bustle of family life, Kate had longed for a few hours on her own, so she could think a little more clearly. But now the time had come, she could only feel the loneliness of her position.

And now her stepmother ran Hazelbank so efficiently, there was not really enough for her to do here. Although she enjoyed her job in the post office, sometimes it was very much a matter of routine, and she often felt she was growing out of the work she had to do.

Carefully Kate pressed the tiny pink garments she had knitted for baby Alison, and wrapped them in tissue paper, then fancy gift paper.

She shouldn't be so depressed about

her own affairs, she told herself severely, when she had so much to be thankful for.

Gemma and the baby were now home, and both were doing well. And her father looked stronger and more confident every day.

Packing everything into a large carrier bag, she locked up the house and set off along the quiet road to Meadowpark.

Caroline Reid was delighted to see Kate when she walked into the large farmhouse kitchen, her cheeks glowing with the exertion of walking.

'I've brought your brown casuals, and your green sweater,' she said, putting down the carrier bag, 'among other things from Sally for Gemma. That bag, by the way, is for Norrie. Some sweets to keep him happy.'

'Thank you, Kate dear,' Caroline said gratefully. 'I must be getting old, or I've been away from the wards too long, but my feet are killing me!

'Not a word to Gemma, though! It

doesn't matter a bit. I'm thoroughly enjoying having a new mother and baby to look after. Still, it's only until Friday, then Moira is coming back. Gemma should be able to do quite a bit herself by then.'

'How are you managing with Norrie?'

'I think we understand one another,' she said, a twinkle in her eye. 'He's a dear little boy underneath all that energy. He's quite in awe of the nurse who comes in. I think it's the uniform. He actually sits down quietly while she sees to the baby.'

They both laughed heartily, then Kate went into the sitting-room where her sister was resting on the settee. The tiny baby girl lay sleeping in her carry-cot while Norrie played quietly with his train set on the rug in front of the fire. Like Sally, Kate felt a wave of emotion at the happy scene.

'Has anyone ever told you you're a very lucky girl?' she asked her sister.

Gemma nodded. 'I know. I'm very happy. Kate. I . . . I only wish . . . '

But the wish remained unspoken between them, and for a long moment Kate was tempted to confide in her sister, assure her that she, too, was happy in her own way.

Then Caroline Reid came in, pushing a trolley, and Norrie got up to help his granny pass round sandwiches and scones.

'I'd better be getting back,' Kate said rather reluctantly, after she had sat by the fire for an hour or two, and nursed the baby when she got too restless in her cot. It was hard to leave the loving warmth and security.

As she walked back to Hazelbank, her mind was busy again with the question of what she should do with her life.

She had thought vaguely about going to London, and had even wondered at one time if she could stay with Sally.

But now Sally was off to Switzerland, and the only other person she knew who had lived for any length of time in London was Angus.

However hard she tried, her thoughts always turned a full circle, and came back to him. She just couldn't put Angus out of her life.

His three months in Brazil would be up now, but he had said nothing to her about future plans.

She was almost certain, however, that he wouldn't wish merely to take up the threads of his life in Stronmore.

Angus's work would take him much farther afield, now that his talent was being recognised.

'Are you going to walk right past me?' Lachie asked teasingly, as Kate walked on, deep in thought. 'You're always doing your best to ignore me.'

'Lachie! Sorry, I was dreaming.'

She stared into his pleasant, smiling face. How well Lachie was looking, thought Kate.

'You look very pleased with yourself,' she commented.

Lachie's ruddy complexion took on a deeper tinge.

'Well, yes.' He grinned rather sheepishly. 'Well, I . . . I've just heard from Moira,' he admitted. 'She's coming back on Friday.'

'I know. Caroline mentioned it. Have you been missing her, Lachie?'

He nodded, his eyes very bright.

'Och, you might as well know, Kate. I asked Moira to marry me, but she wasn't at all sure in her own mind. But now that she's been home again for a few days, it has all been put into perspective for her.

'She . . . she wants to get engaged for a few months, then if we both feel the same way, we'll be getting married by next spring.

'I know I won't change, and I'll see to it that she needn't change her mind, either, so that's one wedding you can look forward to, Kate.'

'Oh, Lachie! I'm so pleased for you,' Kate said, genuine delight in her voice. 'I'm very fond of Moira. I can't think of anyone better for you. You suit one another so well.'

'Thanks, Kate.'

Lachie shuffled about awkwardly.

'Moira knows we've always been friends, Kate.'

'And always will be, I'm sure.' Kate smiled. 'Don't worry, Lachie, I'll see she doesn't get the wrong impression.'

'I never have to explain things to you, do I?'

Lachie glanced at his watch.

'I'll have to hurry on home. Mother and Father are both out tonight, and I promised to stay in, just in case one of us is needed.'

'See you later then,' Kate said.

She longed to ask if he had heard from Angus recently, but her deep reserve stilled her tongue.

In his new happiness, Lachie might want to offer her sympathy because Angus hadn't written to her, and she wanted none. She didn't want anyone to know how much it hurt.

As she neared home, she saw a long sleek grey car drawing up in front of the house, and for a moment she expected some business friend of her father's to climb out.

But the girl who stepped out of the car was tall and very elegant, and Kate recognised her instantly. It was Felicity Powers, whom she had last seen on TV preparing to leave for Brazil along with Angus and the other members of the team.

Kate's mouth felt dry as she hurried forward to greet the other girl.

What could Felicity Powers be doing in Stronmore? Had anything happened to Angus?

Or could it be that Angus was on his way back home and had arranged to meet her in Stronmore? If not, why was the girl here?

Could her interest be such that she wanted to meet Angus's friends, see his home, perhaps make herself known to his parents?

Kate felt unhappy at the prospect. The other girl was so very much more attractive, had so much more in common with Angus, that it seemed to

Kate she could never compete with her for Angus's attention.

* * *

At close quarters, Felicity Powers looked even more beautiful than she had done on television. Her complexion had been darkened a little by warm sunshine, and she glowed with health and vitality.

Her black velvet jacket and swinging skirt were elegantly cut and fitted her to perfection.

'I'm Felicity Powers. Mr Fraser — Angus — said you probably wouldn't mind if I called on you.'

Kate swallowed. 'No of course not,' she said huskily. 'Please . . . please come in. My parents and stepbrother are out, I'm afraid, but I'm sure you'd welcome a cup of coffee.'

'Thanks, I would. I've checked in at the hotel, but I didn't really wait for tea. I've been to Angus's home. That pretty cottage on the hill, isn't it? But there was no-one in, so I came on here.'

'Mr and Mrs Fraser are out for the evening, and Lachie was on his way home when I saw him a moment ago.'

'Oh good. I'll be able to call on him later.'

'How is Angus?' Kate asked, as she prepared a tea tray. She was longing to ask a dozen questions and to know what Angus was doing, but she hesitated to show how very much it mattered to her.

'Oh . . . he's OK,' Felicity Powers said off-handedly.

'He isn't home then?'

'No. Maybe I'd better wait till tomorrow before I call on the Frasers then, if they are going to be home late, I mean.'

'Then you're staying on for a few days?' Kate asked.

'Yes, I expect to stay. I want to do some walking, and take a few photographs. So far I've only driven round the village in my car, but I can recognise most places from Angus's description. It's out of this world!'

'You like it?'

'Like it! I should say so! It looks just wonderful from my point of view, though I hope to get to know it a great deal better.

'It's the kind of place you dream about — if you know what I mean?'

Kate watched the other girl turning to look at the view from the sitting-room window. She had always loved her home, though she had taken the lovely view of fresh green fields with wooded areas, and the heather-clad hills beyond, very much for granted. Now she saw that it did, indeed, look beautiful to Miss Powers.

'Angus said that if I asked you nicely, you might walk round with me, and show me some of his old haunts,' the other girl said, turning to smile at her.

'Kate's mouth felt dry. She could no longer hide from herself just why Miss Powers had come to Stronmore.

It seemed obvious she and Angus must have fallen in love. She must want

324

to get to know Angus's family, his whole background.

Kate took hold of herself as fierce pride once again rose out of the hurt within her.

'Of course I'll show you round, as far as possible,' she agreed, 'though as Angus may have told you, I do work during the day.'

'Oh, that's OK,' said Miss Powers. 'There's a great deal I can do on my own, just getting the feel of the place.

'Brazil was beautiful, but I can well understand why Angus loves his home, and the village. It's all so . . . so fresh, and genuine somehow.'

Felicity Powers certainly had fallen in love with Stronmore, thought Kate, as she listened to the other girl. If only she would tell her a little about Angus.

'How is Angus?' she asked again, breaking in on the other girl's lengthy impressions. 'I haven't had any news of him for some time, and I've rather wondered . . . '

Felicity Powers' manner grew rather cool.

'Oh, I leave it to Angus to get in touch with his friends,' she said, suddenly leaping to her feet. 'Goodness, is that the time? I do seem to have stayed rather long. I'll see you later then, Miss Reid.'

She was gone almost before Kate knew it. She had asked about Angus, and had been well and truly snubbed.

Suddenly she found the tears were running down her cheeks, as she stood with her back to the door.

She could no longer pretend, even to herself. It was all over — Angus was lost to her.

# Family Gathering

The days seemed very long and lonely to Kate, and she welcomed Caroline Reid's return, when she came home to Hazelbank the following weekend.

'Oh, I'm so glad to see you back,' Kate said, a small catch in her voice.

'It's lovely to be back,' Caroline Reid said, though her steady blue eyes were already taking in details of Kate's appearance.

There were deep shadows under the girl's eyes, as though she had been crying herself to sleep at nights, and her small face was very pale.

Caroline Reid realised her stepdaughter was very unhappy, and resolved to speak to her husband about it. Somehow she must try to remove those shadows from Kate's eyes.

'Well, what's been happening?' she asked brightly.

'Oh, nothing much. There's a post-card from Sally. Oh, there's the phone . . . '

'I'll get it,' Caroline said.

Kate sat quietly by the fireside, listening to Caroline's low voice.

'Who is speaking, please? Miss Powers? I see, just a moment, please.'

Kate rose tiredly to her feet as Caroline Reid came into the sitting-room.

'Felicity Powers for you, dear.'

'Yes. I know.'

Her stepmother's eyes were very thoughtful as Kate took the call. Wasn't that the young lady who had been on television with Angus Fraser? She looked enquiringly at Kate when the girl came back into the sitting-room.

'Miss Powers is calling for me at eleven tomorrow morning,' she said. 'I . . . I'm taking her to various places around Stronmore.

'She wants to get to know all Angus's old haunts, and she also wants to see West Lodge, to photograph the work

Angus did on restoring the panelling. Mr Richmond has given her permission, but she'd like me to go with her.'

Caroline Reid's eyebrows drew together. 'Is Angus back home, then?'

'No.' Kate shook her head. 'Apparently he is still very busy. Miss Powers is staying at the hotel.'

There was silence for a moment or two while Caroline fought against rising anger. It was obvious this girl must have some sort of special relationship with Angus Fraser, and that it was hurting Kate to accompany her to all the places she, herself, had shared with him so often in the past.

That evening Mrs Reid had hoped to have a word with her husband, but he and Keith were still deeply absorbed in the plans and costing for the work on Tordale Castle.

Both were anxious, wondering if their estimate had been fair, yet not so high that it would spoil their chances of winning the contract.

'Can't you leave it for a little while?'

Caroline Reid pleaded. 'I want to talk about Kate.'

'What about her?' Gavin Reid asked.

His wife sighed. Perhaps it could all keep until Gavin and Keith received word about the contract, one way or another.

'Never mind, dear,' she said. 'Nothing to worry about for the moment.'

During the following week, Caroline Reid encouraged Kate to help around the house, instead of allowing Felicity Powers to monopolise her. There was plenty for them both to do.

'The baby is going to be christened next Sunday,' she told Kate. 'But although Moira is back helping Gemma, she's so excited because of her engagement that she has little thought for anything else!'

For a moment, Kate's eyes softened and she laughed.

'She and Lachie are very happy,' she said. 'They came into the post office yesterday to post some letters, and Lachie bought a small china pig with flowers on it at our souvenir counter. He says it's for Moira's bottom drawer.'

They both laughed heartily, then Caroline Reid's expression changed and she frowned.

'You know, you could do with a short holiday after the christening, dear. I was wondering how you would feel about spending a few days in London. I have a very old friend — Linda Newman — who has a nice flat in Fulham. We trained together, and we've always kept in touch.'

Kate creamed butter and sugar together, her mind busy.

'I think I would like that, Caroline,' she agreed. 'As a matter of fact, I — I've rather been wondering about a change, a complete change, I mean. Perhaps I could look for a job in London.'

Caroline Reid's eyes grew moist. If Kate went to live in London she would miss her very much.

'Alec and Gemma want to have 'open house' after the christening,' Caroline said, changing the subject completely. 'They want to invite everyone who wants to come back from church to a small buffet celebration. Do you think many people will come?'

'I think we'll have to be prepared for quite a number,' Kate said. 'I'll make another two dozen sausage rolls and vol-au-vents. We've got enough small sponge cakes and biscuits.'

'Judging by the number of cards and christening gifts Alison has collected, we are in for a busy day,' Caroline Reid agreed. 'Don't you think Norrie is very good with the baby? He is so proud of her.'

'He is growing up,' Kate said, glad that things were going so well for her sister. She glanced at the clock.

'I'll leave this for now. I'm taking Felicity Powers to see Peel Hill this morning.'

Caroline's lips firmed, but she said nothing. Nevertheless, she resolved to write to Linda Newman as soon as the christening was over.

\* \* \*

The following Sunday dawned crisp and clear after a rather cold, wet spell. The change of weather seemed to reflect a change of mood in the whole of Stronmore as the church began to fill up with happy, smiling people.

News of Alison's christening, followed by tea at Meadowpark, had quickly passed round the village.

Kate was very touched to see so many people she had known and loved all her life present as she walked into church behind her stepmother, with her father and Keith bringing up the rear.

Alec and Gemma were already at the front of the church, with Moira, as godmother, holding the baby.

Norrie was on his knees beside them, preferring to face the congregation instead of the pulpit, although he spent some of his time gazing adoringly into the tiny face of his new baby sister.

As the organ played softly, Kate looked round, smiling warmly at the

Frasers. Bob and Molly Simpson, old Dr Spiers, and even old Mrs Clark whose cottage had been so beautifully restored by Angus.

Thinking about Angus. Kate again forced back a lump in her throat.

Would she be running away, she wondered, by planning to go to London? Was it a wise move to leave all the people she loved so much in Stronmore?

Kate was unsure and yet she must try to build herself a new life. If she remained here, she would always be living in the past.

There was a rustle throughout the church, and Kate glanced round again, seeing that Felicity Powers had walked down towards the centre of the church, her tall, elegant figure a focus of great interest to the local people.

There had no doubt been a great deal of speculation about her, thought Kate, looking down at her gloved hands.

Then she was on her feet as the

service started, and the small, thin wail of the disturbed baby rose above the hymn singing.

Kate saw a few smiles of sympathy and amusement, then Lachie's proud smile as Moira soon quietened the baby.

Towards the end of the service, Alison was brought forward to be christened, and Kate listened to the words of the minister, her heart full of tenderness.

Would she, she wondered, be able to return to Stronmore one day with her own child, and listen to these same age-old words? Deep down, she had always hoped that one day, she and Angus . . .

There was a slight commotion at the back of the church, and Kate looked round, her heart seeming to stop for a moment.

Angus had just walked into the church and was slipping quietly into a back pew.

Even as she watched, Kate could see

how thin and gaunt he looked, his face almost yellowish in pallor.

Her thoughts reeling, she turned back automatically as the organ swelled, and the congregation began to sing the last hymn.

After the service, Kate lost little time in following Angus out of church. The sight of his thin figure had put all thoughts of Felicity Powers out of her head, and the one thing which was uppermost in her mind was to find him and to find out what was wrong.

He was waiting for her near an ancient beech tree at the side of the church, where they had often played together as children.

Kate ran towards him, her eyes anxious.

'Angus! What has happened?' She gasped. 'Oh . . . Angus!'

His arms were as strong as ever when he pulled her to him, holding her close.

'Don't panic, darling,' he said. 'I didn't want you to know, and believe me, I'm all right now. I'm well on the mend.'

'But . . . '

'It was a bug. Trust me to pick up something! It laid me low for a few weeks while I was still in Brazil.'

'But why didn't you tell me?' she asked.

'You had so much to worry about already,' Angus told her. 'With your father ill, and Gemma, and . . . and the business. I just couldn't add to your worries, Kate.'

'Oh, Angus! I — I've been so worried. I thought . . . '

She broke off, remembering Felicity Powers, but again Angus was holding her tightly, having seen her love for him shining from her eyes.

'Perhaps it was wrong of me, but never mind. It's all in the past now, Kate, don't let's waste any more time. Let's get married soon. I've missed you so much.'

Kate's eyes were shining like stars.

'Of course I'll marry you, Angus.'

Angus smiled down at her. 'Kate, I'm so happy. I think I've always loved you.'

'I know that I've loved you all my life, Angus.' Kate said softly. 'I didn't know it was possible to be this happy. For a while I wasn't sure, you see.'

'Wasn't sure?'

'No, but that is all in the past, too, Angus. You're home, darling, and everything is wonderful.'

★ ★ ★

For a few more moments they were alone, the rest of the world shut out, then Kate turned round as she heard the sound of footsteps behind her.

Felicity Powers was walking towards them, a smile of welcome on her face.

'Hello, Angus,' she said. 'So you got here OK. Hold still for a moment, while I take a picture of both of you.'

'Can't you stop working, even for a moment?' Angus asked teasingly. 'This is a private moment for Kate and me. We've just got engaged.'

'Better and better,' Felicity said. 'I've loads of pictures for the brochure my father is preparing, by the way.'

'What brochure?' Kate asked.

Felicity turned to her with a smile.

'I forgot that you don't really know about it,' she said, falling into step beside them. 'It was all very confidential until the whole project was finished, but Father knew that Angus's work is going to arouse a lot of interest, and he has prepared a brochure on the artist.

'I've had to build up a picture of Angus's background for the public.'

She put an arm through Kate's. 'I'm sorry I couldn't discuss it freely with you, Kate dear, but I was scared I would say the wrong thing. Angus had asked me not to mention that he'd picked up that awful bug.

'We were all very worried about him at one time, though he's OK now. You see how it was, though. I really had to be careful what I told you!'

'I . . . I see,' Kate said weakly.

'But let's forget all that. Congratulations, both of you.'

'Well, thank you,' Kate said, while

Angus again hugged her to him.

'She isn't really so bad,' he said, grinning.

'Please keep one more secret, just for a short while,' Kate said to Felicity. 'We'll have to tell our families about our engagement. They will want to hear our news before everyone does.'

Felicity smiled with understanding.

'I'm rather better now at keeping secrets,' she said. 'Shall we all go to Meadowpark in my car? I could use a cup of tea, and some of those savouries you were making, Kate.'

'Then the sooner we get there, the better,' Kate said, looking at her watch. 'I'm on duty behind Gemma's large brown teapot!'

She turned to give Angus a radiant smile and Felicity's eyes were full of amusement. She had thought that Kate Reid was a quietly pretty girl, but now she saw that Kate was indeed beautiful.

There would be no need for her to keep the engagement secret for very long. It was all there for people to read on the faces of both Angus and Kate.

The following day. Felicity Powers left again for London, though Angus was staying at home for another week before he, too, would have to go back to London.

For Kate the days seemed to pass in a golden haze. As Felicity had predicted, news of their engagement soon leaked out, after Kate and Angus had told their respective families, and the whole village seemed to rejoice with them.

'I thought I was never going to see my sons settled,' Mary Fraser said happily. 'And now I'm about to acquire two daughters-in-law, one after the other.'

'We just took our time, and chose well,' Lachie said solemnly, and his mother smiled, deeply thankful to see both her sons happy.

The families were planning a small party at Hazelbank the following Saturday, before Angus had to leave for London.

He had already talked for a long time

with Mr Reid, giving him a great many particulars about his plans for the future.

'Kate will have to travel with me quite a lot,' Angus said. 'Already I've been offered other commissions, some of them abroad. She says she doesn't mind the travelling, Mr Reid.'

'I'm sure it will be a good life for both of you, and there's plenty of time for you to settle down, if you want to in the future.'

For a long time he was silent, thinking of the changes that lay ahead, then he sighed. He was no longer afraid of change. It hadn't always been for the better, but it had always been a challenge.

He thought about his wife, and was deeply grateful as he recognised where a great deal of the strength to fight had come from.

'You must never be afraid of the future, so long as you are together, Angus,' Gavin Reid said, and the younger man nodded with deep understanding.

Two days later, the contract for

Tordale Castle arrived on Gavin Reid's desk, and this time it was Keith who really shared his stepfather's joy and satisfaction.

'We would have put the company straight now, anyway,' he said, 'but this puts the seal on our efforts. Just wait till we tell Mother and Kate.'

Gavin Reid smiled. 'Sometimes they like to spring surprises on us,' he said. 'Let's keep this under our hats until Saturday evening, shall we?'

'A good idea,' Keith agreed.

His own satisfaction at landing the contract was quite enough for him.

\* \* \*

On Saturday evening, Caroline thought she had never seen Kate looking more beautiful.

Caroline Reid had deliberately kept her own dress simple, wanting it to be Kate's evening, though she had to admit that Moira, too, looked beautiful when she arrived with Lachie.

Gemma and Alec had decided to have a quiet night on their own, with their small family.

'Gemma says she'll bring the children tomorrow.' Moira said.

'They'll pay a quiet visit in the afternoon. At the moment she's had enough excitement.'

'Very sensible,' Caroline said, and then hurried off to welcome Mr and Mrs Fraser and Angus, who had no eyes for anyone but Kate as she ran forward to greet him.

Earlier in the evening, Sally had telephoned her congratulations, and Kate was still glowing after her cheerful conversation with her sister.

'Sally sends her love,' she told Angus. 'She's well settled in Switzerland, and enjoying her course.'

It was a very happy gathering that sat down to eat the delicious meal Caroline had prepared, with the help of Mrs Simpson.

She would remember it all her life, thought Kate, as she looked round at all her family, and felt Angus reaching for her hand, and holding it as though he would never let her go.

Gavin Reid rose to his feet and the hum of conversation died down as he began to speak.

'I can't tell you what joy it gives me to see a family gathering of this kind,' he began, 'and to toast the future happiness of Kate and Angus, also Moira and Lachie.'

The happy laughter broke out again, then Gavin Reid turned to his stepson.

'Also to Keith,' he said, 'whose skill and competence has helped to land Reid's the contract for the renovation of Tordale Castle . . . '

'Gavin!' his wife cried reproachfully. 'And to think you never told me!'

Gavin Reid turned to her, and she could see love and gratitude in his eyes.

'No. This time I decided to surprise you, my dear,' he said gently, 'because without you, none of it would have been possible.'

Gavin Reid took his wife's hand and raised his glass.

'To you, my dear,' he said, and Caroline knew that her cup of happiness was full.

## THE END